What Sort of Man

Also by Breton Dukes

Bird North *and other stories*

Empty Bones *and other stories*

What Sort of Man

and other stories

BRETON DUKES

Victoria University of Wellington Press

Victoria University of Wellington Press
PO Box 600, Wellington
New Zealand
vup.wgtn.ac.nz

First published 2020

A catalogue record is available from the
National Library of New Zealand.

ISBN 9781776563029

Published with the assistance of a grant from

Printed by Ligare, Auckland

Contents

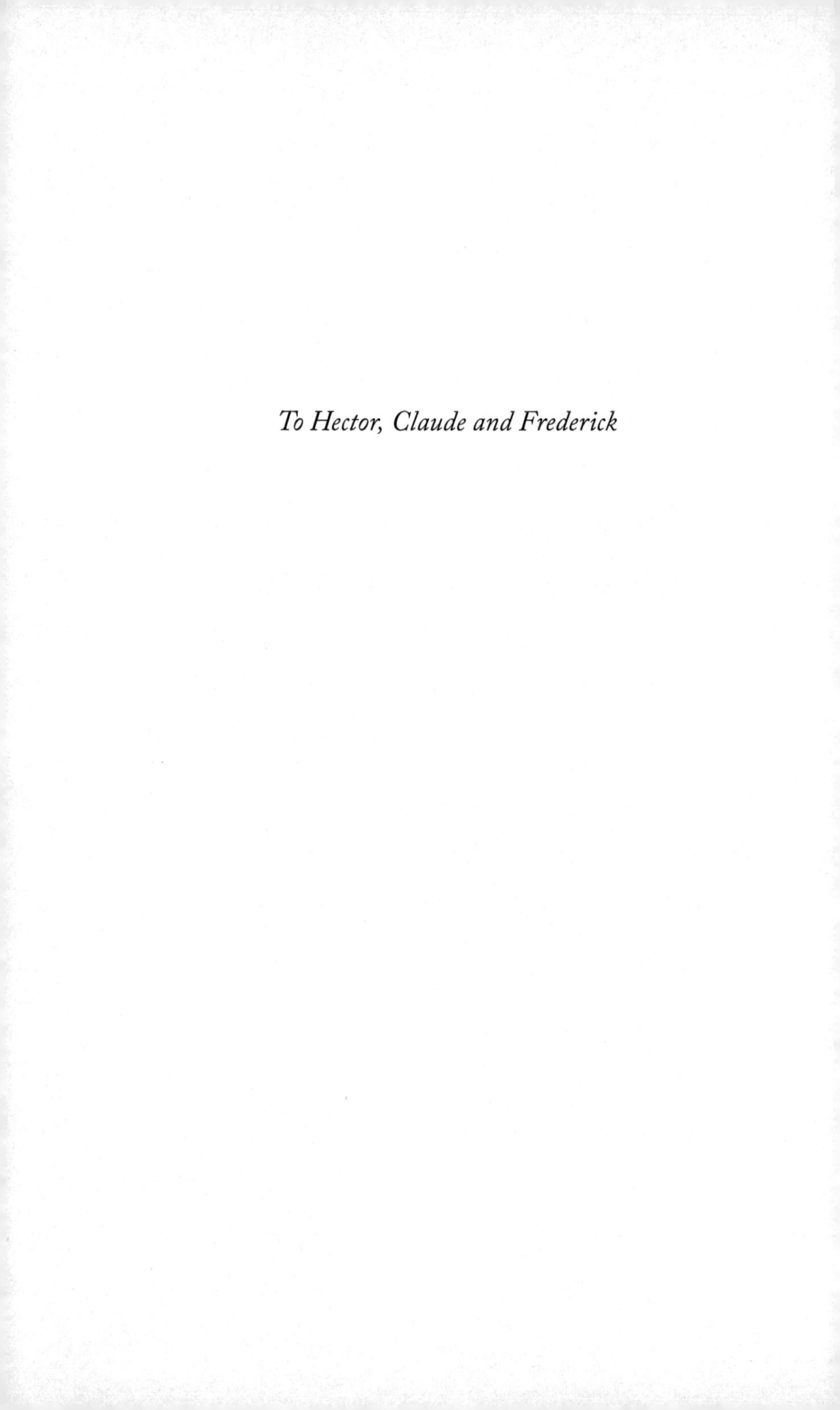

To Hector, Claude and Frederick

Ross Creek

When Melanie was two, Kelly got a good job at the university and Gary took a year off. They'd just bought a house that was big and old and his plan was to get into some DIY: replacing weatherboards, painting, wallpapering, building a deck, while also caring for Melanie. What he found, though, was that a two-year-old requires one hundred per cent monitoring, and though she'd nap in the afternoons, Gary, tired from tidying away big pools of toys, making peanut-butter soldiers, getting her from one outfit—a cowgirl, say—into another—a frog princess—and then going out to look for worm kingdoms or play gutter-boats, would, by then, be buggered. So, none of what he'd planned to do that year got done.

'But do you see that that didn't matter, Melanie?' says Gary, talking intensely into the phone. 'Redecorating or whatever wasn't what that year was about. That year was about developing this amazing relationship with you, my little girl.'

Down the line Melanie—now seventeen—says coldly, 'Right, Dad.'

He nudges the toast on his plate. 'Did you drop off this marmalade, love?'

She doesn't say anything, just carefully hangs up, as

though it—the hanging up—is what she wants him to take from the call.

It's a week since the stuff was found on Gary's computer and he's at the kitchen table of the house he rented. There's the *ODT* and now the phone which he stands beside the plate of toast he's spread with the marmalade he found when he went for the newspaper. Trump and North Korea are front page, Snow Expected to Low Levels, Sex Attack in the Botanic Gardens—following an earlier incident in the same location, police now have concerns about a serial offender. Women are advised to avoid the area at night. Police patrols are being considered. So are CCTV cameras.

Gary eats and looks through the rest of the paper, but it's hard to concentrate and before getting to the sports pages he refolds it—so he's facing the front page again—and shifts the wooden chair back from the table. Then what he does is sink his chin to his chest and stare through his toes at the unfamiliar lino.

'Questionable files?' Kelly had said.

Melanie had been crouched on the couch, looking into her knees.

'Pornography? *Porn*?' Kelly said.

The way she said it got Melanie standing.

Gary hadn't said anything—what could he say?—just tried to hug his daughter, who shoved him away and stood, tilted forward like her mum, ready to fight.

'Nothing illegal,' Gary said, actually holding up his hands as if one of them had a gun. 'Just some photos.'

Melanie started shivering like the news was iced water he'd drenched her in.

Kelly pointed at Gary and then the front door. 'Out,' she said.

Those first few nights, Gary stayed in a motel. Now he's in this shoebox on Opoho Road, ten minutes' drive from his little family and their house in Belleknowes. Though they might as well be in Pyongyang. No one answers their cell phones, the landline's been disconnected—just now he'd been talking to Melanie via the secretary at her high school—and probably Kelly's changed the locks, probably she's set up her own CCTV and called in the cops to patrol outside his old house.

Thirty years he's been teaching. He gets good ERO. New teachers seek him out for advice on tricky students or tricky modules. Pupils know they can have a joke even a crude one—just as they know there's a line not to cross. And now what? The principal won't return his calls, no one from the staffroom answers his texts. Will he be fired? Deregistered? Is he getting divorced?

Kelly obviously knows where he's living—the marmalade. Or was it Melanie? At least she's still attending school. Lately she's been sensitive about him being a teacher—hating it when he asked knowing questions about trends and fads, hating his *feeling* for teenage girls. When other people find out—Dunedin's a small place—she'll be humiliated. If she'd just agree to see him . . . Though she won't talk to him on the phone, so how's he going to do that? He knows the route she takes walking home from school—maybe he should wait somewhere along the way? As her dad, hasn't he earned the right to explain? But even when he has talked to her, will they have to leave? He taught for a few years in Blenheim once, but otherwise he's always lived here.

A wood pigeon—from the Botanic Gardens no doubt; the house abuts its western boundary—bombs over his house and down towards Knox College. Red-brick and big, with steeples and flags like a castle.

Or jail. Though there's been no mention of the police. He hasn't broken the law, has he? Far as he knows the whole mess is with the Teachers' Complaints Assessment Committee.

What he would like made clear—what he'd especially like to tell Kelly and Melanie—is:

1. He only ever looked *after* school.
2. He always locked the classroom door.
3. All he did was look.

'Not like this guy,' Gary says aloud, scanning the article about the assaults.

In the upper part of the Botanic Gardens, Gary's in his running gear—shorts, long johns, running shoes, a windbreaker. It's quiet, but for his feet on the pebbled path. Ahead a blackbird stitches at the wet grass on the side of the track. It's still and damp and around Gary the tall pines arrow up, touching their tips into drifts of fog.

After finishing with the newspaper he'd texted Melanie twice and called Kelly. But of course she didn't answer, and even though he's written out his bullet points and practised delivering them in a calm, sure way, he didn't leave a message.

At a sign that points up towards the aviary and the

rhododendron dell, and down towards the rotunda and playground, he stops. He scans back down the path and then rotates, looking up into the bank of pines and then eucalyptus. Damp and still—the grass between the trees is longer, there are dirt tracks where people walk. Up is the way he'll go—after all the sitting he's been doing, the exercise feels good in his legs. Why doesn't he start running again? After the investigation, or whenever . . . Really, what's the big deal about a few film clips and photos? Really, what man with an internet connection hasn't looked?

Ahead, there's the sound of something and Gary goes off the track—across the wet grass, scaring off the blackbird—and behind one of the pines with its python-sized roots. Some people are proud of their eyesight—20/20 and all that—but Gary's always gloated about his hearing. As a teacher, it's a serious advantage—catching all that classroom whispering—and so now he relaxes towards the faint noise: footsteps on the path, more than one set, two people at least, two men, laughing.

It's true, what he'd said to Melanie about their relationship. He loved that year. It was tedious and hard, and the imbalance with Kelly earning and him doing all the parenting was hard on the marriage, but he'd started the year not really *knowing* Melanie, not knowing the intricacies of her personality, and by the end, when she went off to day-care and he returned to teaching, he felt they'd established something long-lasting and important.

The men have passed—their conversation trickling after them—and Gary gets up, comes out from behind the tree and re-crosses the grass. He's been a good dad. That's what Melanie needs to understand. Everyone has good and bad in their personality. But if you can shepherd your children, if you can work hard and devote yourself to your partner . . .

'I've done okay,' he whispers, starting up the track towards where advanced hearing isn't required to understand that one of the aviary's parrots has just curdled the gloom with a terrible cry.

Kelly only likes soap. Mannish sort of stuff like Palmolive Gold. So, shower gel's one good thing about not being at home and Gary goes about lathering his hairy legs with the lime-green stuff. While down there, though, he starts crying for his old life: the smell of their bedroom—somehow the incense they used to burn has permeated the walls; Kelly's winter porridge: wholegrain oats, raisins, cream, brown sugar.

One morning, at the end of last century, Kelly brought him an earlier version of that porridge on a tray with orange juice, coffee and a vase. Instead of a rose, the vase held a positive pregnancy test. The thick + of it looking out from the glass. They'd screwed and screwed at the right time of the month for years, but nothing had happened. Two cycles of IVF had failed, and earlier that very week they'd met a woman about adoption—you chose Romania or Thailand—but in the end, no need! Regulation sex, in their incense-smelling bedroom, worked. And after eight-and-a-bit months, long-footed, 2.8kg Melanie Anne Simpson arrived.

Those big feet! They must help her running—at the moment she's training for the Dunedin Half Marathon. Standing, he gets hold of his crying. They could run it together—didn't they talk about it a few months back? He's been so busy lately, but suddenly there's all this time. Whatever else happens it would be something positive to share.

Trying to get his mouth into the shape you need for whistling, Gary starts soaping his arms. He's lost everyone else, but he's not losing Melanie.

Gary lights up the little carport with his car's headlights. He *is* going to see Melanie. She hasn't responded to his texts and her email bounced his message straight back. Probably Kelly's dug all their daughter's technology in with the potatoes. Probably she's got Melanie on some sort of curfew. Because when he waited for her after school—he'd parked up the hill a bit, next to the playground with the tall trees—among all those girls from Kavanaugh and Otago Girls', there was no Melanie. Maybe she'd gone home at lunchtime. Maybe his phone call had upset her. She wasn't wagging, was she? Sixteen years of parenting and now he's the invisible man?

No. No chance.

And so, getting home from his stake-out, he ate more toast, slept, and showered again, waiting out the rest of the day. Too early and Kelly might still be up, too late and it'll be Melanie who'll be asleep. Swivelled in the car seat, he reverses out onto Opoho Road.

On the radio, they're talking about a new attack: a

body found in the upper part of the Botanic Gardens. Detectives from around Otago are flooding Dunedin. The victim has been identified, but no name—or any other details—will be available until the family's been notified. Police will issue a statement later in the day, but in the meantime, for the first time ever, the Botanic Gardens are, without exception, closed. Tomorrow, Mayor Hawkins, city councillors and Dunedin's two Members of Parliament will meet with police, and representatives from the university. A Facebook page promoting a Reclaim the Night march has been established. Student Health has beefed up its roster of counsellors and all North Dunedin schools will close until the end of the week.

'Mayor Hawkins,' says Gary. 'Member of Parliament,' he says, rolling his tongue around the different titles. Logan Park High will be closed. It would have been the sort of thing Gary got consulted on. A high school is a tiny world within the world and Gary used to be near the peak of its hierarchy. Not just as a senior teacher, but as a senior teacher with serious mana. Getting a green at the Gardens corner he coasts through, towards more lights—shivering red and blue—and high-vis people signalling, walking forward, waving with hands and torches.

He pulls over and stops where the cop—a woman—indicates. When he runs his window down, the air stirs the shower-gel smell through the car.

In her vest, police beanie, and jacket, she says, 'Good evening, sir.'

'Hi,' says Gary.

'You've heard what happened in the Gardens?'

Gary's aware his hands are gripping the wheel. Nodding, he casually lets them fall into his lap.

'Okay there, sir?'

Years of dealing with cunning students have trained Gary in the right way to handle interrogation. You want to appear a little guilty—everyone does under questioning—then you pivot to something deeply personal, even a little embarrassing, though 'I've got a young daughter of my own' will do here.

'Mr Simpson?' says the officer, crouching lower.

It happens a lot. Ex-pupils. He's been at it so long there's often generations of students in the same family. Some of them he remembers—but not this one with her cheekbones and close-set eyes.

'Tania Kershaw,' she says. 'I was Miller back then.'

Gary smiles sadly. 'Any luck, Tania?'

Something about the way she says 'We'll get him' clicks up the memory of an earnest Year 12.

'Good,' says Gary, as though they're in class and she's telling him about some project she's putting extra effort into.

'You haven't seen or heard anything unusual?'

Next rule: don't say too much. So Gary just shrugs, smiles, and re-grips the wheel. Taking it as her cue, Tania smiles into the car then pushes away from his door.

In his side and then rear-vision mirror, Gary watches her walk towards the next vehicle, signalling.

Melanie was seven when she ran away to the St Clair pool. She'd demanded they go and when Gary said no she slipped out of the house with her togs, walked down into town, and caught the bus along here, along George Street, along Princes Street, through South Dunedin, all the way to the route's termination, two minutes' walk from the Pacific and the salt-water pool.

There was an hour of panic, and frantic rushing, then Gary called the pool, and yes, a young girl had gone through, saying her auntie was inside.

In the car, going to collect her, Kelly worried they'd spoilt her too much, had squeezed her too close, and now she'd shot away from them like a fruit pip.

'Maybe she was hot and just wanted a swim?' Gary remembers saying.

Kids ran off, but wouldn't she have been scared? Out in the world? With the worn-down South Dunedin types that rode the rattly buses?

Later, after a telling-off, when Gary had asked her those questions, Melanie had shaken her head, smiled at him over her ice cream, and run through the steps she'd taken. Money from the jar on Dad's dresser, her togs bag, past the house with the red door, past the playground with the tall trees, down the long road, into town . . . Fear, any sort of emotion was blanked by the practical requirements of her mission. Which, as a teacher, was something Gary taught. Facing a challenge, something hard or unpleasant, something shit-scary—that always got a laugh, occasionally it's good to talk at their level—break the task into practical steps. And then begin.

Which for Gary means getting out of his car and going through the wrought-iron gate, up the four steep steps and along the path curving darkly around the front of his old, two-storey villa.

No lights at the front, which is good. The front rooms upstairs are spare so he'd expect them to be dark, but their room downstairs is where Kelly will be. Drawn curtains, zero light at their edges. He keeps walking, his windbreaker rustling where his wrists catch against his hips.

He's in his running clothes, but should he be dressed differently? Normal day clothes? Even a tie? He's always worn one at school. But this time of night what's he going to look like up a ladder in a tie? Working around the house on any average weekend this is basically what he'd wear, so climbing up the ladder to her room, Melanie would expect him dressed like this. *All I did, love, was look at a few pictures. And less than a handful of live feeds.*

His heart comes up—telling your teenage daughter you might be deregistered for accessing teenage porn. But those are details—teenage/live feed—that don't need sharing. Despite all the politically correct stuff going around these days, kids don't always need *all* information. And anyway, remember, this is only about getting up the path and around the corner of the house without Kelly seeing.

And so, his right shoe squeaking, he creeps to the corner of the house. From there he can view the kitchen. It's dark too, with just, from something, a soft blue light—as if with him gone the first thing they've done is buy an aquarium. He takes the next step, sort of limping, trying to keep the weight off the squeaky shoe and here his elbow muscles flicker: twenty years he's been rounding this corner and raising his arm for the door handle. Instead, bending, sort of crab-walking—he wouldn't put it past Kelly to be sitting there in the dark—he gets himself below the window and to the next corner, where he stands and sees all the familiar shapes and surfaces of his backyard.

Once or twice, over the years, Kelly's told him he can be too full-on, even scary. *Leave Mr Bloody Simpson at school*, she says. Sometimes she shouts it. He knows he's expert at crowd control, and giving clear instructions, and that in just walking into a classroom he gives off this air of expectation about the way people should behave. At the same time, she's always ruled the house. What intimidates Gary is her speed, clearing the dishwasher, say, making him feel slow and useless and maybe—and this only comes to him now—what actually makes him angry is his resentment at the deficient feelings she causes him to have about himself. Maybe there are times he's treated Kelly more like a child than an adult, but that's because she's always made him feel like a child.

That's not in play now, though. What's frightening about knowing she's scared are the reactions he's seen when this dynamic plays among students—the scared one often overreacts, getting really violent in the expectation that the scary one will bring their own serious violence . . . But, again, those thoughts aren't helping. The next task is the shed—get in there, get the long ladder, get it up against the house.

Past the low plaster-cast wall they painted last Christmas, and up to the shed door. He pulls on the handle, holding tight while leaning in, wanting the door opened without much sound, and his effort pays off—the door gives quietly to the lawnmower's dried grass and petrol smell. It's dark, but he can see the ladder and his muscles remember the required movements for extraction. Smaller muscles are needed to keep it balanced, and as he stands he makes little puffs of breath as he backs down the steps, down the shed's short path. Then, raising the ladder, he swivels, resting it against the weatherboards on one side of Melanie's window. It's dark there, her curtains are drawn—he'll climb and tap like a boyfriend would, like a lover.

Here's the second rung, in each hand the cold sides of the ladder, and the weight of his foot on the third rung which causes the ladder's tip to shift against the weatherboards. It's a matter of climbing, tapping, waiting, and then, when she comes, smiling and indicating that she should open the window. He's still her dad. He's made a mistake. Everyone makes them—when she gets older she'll find that out for sure. Be firm, but warm, and then, why not, when all that's clear, mention running together. With every interaction, no matter how negative, Gary has always strived to insert something positive, to leave each student with something light and good.

Melanie wakes. Mum is right there, breathing. And there, the tap-tapping that woke her. Water dripping? Something upstairs? Pressing off the pillow she adjusts her head, trying to find the direction. Tap tap-tap. Like something small trying to get free. It stops. What was it? Nothing, probably nothing.

It pisses her off that her heart's going and trying to be casual about it she lies on her back, stretching her legs. But there, there it is again. Re-starting. Louder this time—like someone's tapping on a window and now, with nothing happening, trying for the attention of someone inside, they're tapping harder. It stops again, but the silence seems to swell, holding her down on the mattress.

At school everyone's almost excited about this sex-predator guy, and it's easy to laugh when you're in groups, when you're out in bright sun, but, in the dark . . . Outside the duvet the air is cold on her bare arms and she buries them beneath, feeling with her brain down the back of her right leg, trying to concentrate on checking if the hamstring twinge is still there. She isn't scared.

'I'm not,' she says, using her mouth to shape the words, but not making a sound.

It helps—if she was in her own bed what she'd do is check her phone for the time and any updates online, but Mum wouldn't let her bring it, her *device,* into the room.

The noise has definitely stopped. Probably rats in the walls, maybe a possum on the roof over her room. But still, Melanie wriggles further down the bed, moving a little closer to Mum. Dad's smell off the duvet, probably his hair and all that's in here as well. But so what? You come down your mum's tubes and stuff, so lying in here close with her—where her and Dad got it on all those years—that's nothing. Which was pretty much the skeleton of the conversation they had last night when Mum first suggested Melanie sleep here.

'It's no big deal. Just, with everything going on, I'd like if you kept me company overnight.'

'You mean sleep in your bed?'

'Yes.'

'Then why not just say that?'

Melanie looks at the ceiling where the plaster is shaped into whorls around the light shade. The noise hasn't happened for a while now and she closes her eyes. Dad, like, sitting in his class with his pants around his knees, looking at girls strip and do whatever. Dad rubbing his dick.

Melanie swallows. Beside the bed she'd normally have her Hydrator, but last night they were talking and then she must have slept, so there's no water—and come the morning, whatever Mum says, she's doing a hard run at Ross Creek.

'Just don't overdo it.'

'What does that mean?'

'Don't run too hard. Don't hurt yourself.'

'Too hard?'

'Jesus, Melanie. Over-training. You know what I mean.'

A couple of years ago Mum and Dad went through this major period of, like, capital A arguing. Every single thing: putting rubbish out, the right way to wash the new frying pan, who hadn't paid the phone bill. Melanie stopped it one day by going through the house with a trowel and breaking every window in the house. Even—she's looking through it now—the big one in the kitchen. Like ice, glass shards went down into the sink.

Testing her hamstring, she flexes her foot towards her bum and fills the bottle, empties it, and then fills it again. It's good to be up. Moving helps squash the fear. And her leg feels strong, she feels strong. Out the window is the dark. Just the dark and the shape of the trees. 'The Art of Destruction', Dad had called her after her 'glazing' efforts. He was always fun to play with, the way he put things, the way he could make up games and keep them going with the funny language he'd invent. Flexing and re-flexing, she drinks cold water. The kissing sound of the lino when she flexes, raising her foot. The buzz off the battery charger Mum brought home a few days ago. Within the shapes of the trees and the hedge she can make out the shape of her short hair in the window, and then, a fish passing, it's Dad. Bent low, but not low enough, there and then gone, swimming by.

What Gary wanted to tell Melanie, the bad stuff and the brighter colours he also wanted to paint for her, is caught in his gut, so he doesn't feel right going back to Opoho yet. All that energy spent getting up that ladder and then no release. He's always taught progress to his students—that any progress is better than nothing, even if it gets you further into a mistake.

'Strive, my little mice,' he says now, which was a thing he used to say to some of his smarter junior classes.

Where he is now is Dundas Street, taking an easy drive through Studentville. Over a wide judder bar, across the Leith Stream bridge, past a side entrance to the Gardens where, yes, a police car is parked. Not that the students aren't about! There, two women walking. And there . . . a man in a cap walking up the black snake Lovelock Ave makes against the Gardens.

Up the hill and over—from the crest the view is across

the roofs of flats to the Logan Park sports fields—and here, another figure on the footpath, this time a young woman alone, smoking.

Without thinking, maybe he just wants to see if she'll look, Gary puts his foot on the clutch and revs. But she's occupied with her smoke and the careful way she's walking, as if the footpath is moated on each side by shark-filled waters.

'Crocodiles,' goes Gary. 'Piranhas,' he says, letting out the clutch, driving on.

Logan Park's previous principal, Marshall Tiller, was keen on running, and for a while there—back before Melanie was born—Gary and Marshall used to do lunchtime runs. Marshall was tall and skinny with lots of hair—Hairy Pencil (HP) was what the younger teachers called him behind his back—and as soon as the two of them hit the Gardens, Marshall would be looking around for young women walking to and from the university to buzz. Running past real close, but not touching. Just brushing the sleeve of a T-shirt, say. *Giving some young tail a bit of wind* was the way Marshall put it.

'Let's buzz those two,' he'd say, and off they'd go.

It wasn't like they did it endlessly, just once or twice every run. And they never talked about it—what would they say? But it was definitely part of their running dynamic. Part of why they ran together. Sometimes you got close enough to catch certain *deep* smells—that was back when Gary and Kelly were trying to get pregnant and he found the days he and Hairy went running were the days he went home with the hottest libido.

Parking now, hard against the footpath, down where Dundas Street goes flat—the same street he and Marshall would run to get to the Gardens—Gary kills the headlights and sits back, watching in the rear-vision mirror.

Melanie locks Mum's car with the red button on the key ring then sets the keys on top of the driver's tyre.

'Don't do the thing Dad does with the keys.'

'Right, Mum.'

'Stay away from bush. Stay away from North Dunedin.'

'No bush, no North Dunedin.'

The kettle had been boiling hard and Mum was there in the kitchen flicking through the paper as if the sex fiend had been at it overnight and somehow the reporters had already got it printed.

'For sex fiend updates you'd best go online,' Melanie said, using her Siri voice.

Mum looked up with a hard face, but didn't comment. What she definitely didn't appreciate was Kelly using 'sex fiend' to describe both Dad and the dude rampaging around North Dunedin. But instead of rising to that Mum continued into her seventeenth year of advice/instruction: 'What about the beach at St Clair? There'll be people walking their dogs.'

'Sure, Mum.'

'Don't muck with me, Melanie.'

Now Melanie evolves fast walking into gentle jogging. Around the Ross Creek reservoir is a 1.2km oval of basically flat gravel track. Bush one side, water the other. There's the water tower thingy with its narrow walkway.

Wooden seats where people can have lunch or whatever. Some native birds, but really more of the others: standard ducks, sparrows, blackbirds. Dog-walkers carrying the shit their dogs do in plastic bags that someone—a dog-shit-hater—ties in clusters on a sign by the car park. Usually lots of runners too. Tracks and roads lead in and out around the reservoir—all of it's only five minutes' drive from any number of Central and North Dunedin suburbs. But today the car park is empty and, so far, no dogs or dog-walkers, and no runners. Still, the track, the bush, and the water are here—the calm water's trapping the sky's low cloud. And now at the wooden rubbish bin—as is usual at this part of her warm-up—Melanie lengthens her stride.

These last two weeks, what she's been doing is one lap to warm up and then five laps as fast as she can. Mum and Dad think she's training for the Dunedin Half Marathon, but fuck that, slogging away forever around the harbour with all those bearded old harriers. What she's getting off on lately is speed. Sustained speed. How fast can she cover 6 ks.

Relaxing her jaw, passing the water tower—what's it for, with its windows like a little house?—and getting onto the bend near where the track down to the Leith Valley emerges she pushes harder, leaning into the curve, turning up gravel, scattering small birds that disappear into the bush, sounding their alarms. After her warm-up lap, back near where she parked, she'll do some stretching, then, screw the hamstring, she's going after her PB.

Having decided that—not that there was ever doubt—and not wanting to burn out, she comes off the accelerator as she starts down the back straight part of her circuit, where, instead of running by the water, you've got the bush on one side and this deep, broad overflow drain on the other. The track's wide and you'd have to be drunk to fall in, but what about, like, oldies and the disabled? Couldn't they plop in easily enough? They'd break a hip, they'd crack their skull—and even if they didn't, how would they get out? There's no ladders or anything. What's surprising is that there aren't, like, skeletons down there, of people who have starved it out. At school this sort of hazard would be marked by at least a thousand cones. There'd be a special assembly, drills, letters to take home.

Spitting, Melanie checks her form—head still and tall, like there's fishing line stapled from her head to the sky—and slows further. At the end of her last run, two days ago, she threw up. Went from hands on knees, to sitting, to rolling onto her side and chundering. Nothing major, just a friendly little spew. Mum didn't need to know—she'd have shat out her eyes. If Dad had been around, she might have told him—he'd have been proud—but he's up there in Opoho doing . . .

Melanie holds her forehead for a moment, damming her brain. What would be even better than running is rotoring through the bush—her arms great blades, felling all the fucking trees. Now, with Dad in mind, she works hard to keep her speed down. *Fucking Dad.* What *was* he doing last night? Checking on the lawnmower? Saying gidday to Mum's old bike?

Christ. Why is no one around? Is it the sex fiend they're afraid of? All those poor busting dogs! People, he operates in the Gardens! Though aren't they closed? Remembering the fear-surge from last night, Melanie feels a little of it again and her eyes creep to the trunks of the trees and the low branches at the side of the track. Some pervert watching her, some dude jumping out and grabbing her throat. #RossCreekRapist. She spits again—#Bullshit—letting her jaw flap—#PersonalBest—concentrating on flowing over the gravel.

It was after her puke that she'd decided to take the marmalade. She'd been thinking about Dad and Mum and how he would get it—what she was doing to herself—while Mum wouldn't have a clue. She lives life with so much energy—just watch her vacuuming—that she doesn't have any need for exercise.

There isn't a real bend at the end of the back straight, just a sort of drifting wiggle to the car park and, having regained control of her thinking, Melanie slows to a fast walk. Ahead is the little bridge, covered in licheny stuff, over a stream, and then, up a little, through the dark fingers the tree branches make, there's Mum's car. What Melanie hasn't said to Mum—but is ready to say, ready to scream, really—is that as long as she can keep running fast like this, every day, to yes, the point of puking, while still keeping up all her usual stuff at school, as well as holding on to the hard edges of her attitude/humour, then maybe she can keep convincing everyone—herself especially—that what's happening with Dad isn't ripping her heart apart.

*

'Overnight in Dunedin, police say the 0800 number set up to capture information about recent sex attacks was inundated with missing-person calls. People, they say, are understandably wary, but before calling 111, friends and family are asked to be thorough in exhausting all modes of communication. Area Commander John Guthrie also wants young people, particularly students, to be mindful of parents living outside of Dunedin.

'"If you're a student in Dunedin please respond to parents' calls and texts. We know as a young person this isn't always a priority, but now is the time to check in at least once a day." Commander Guthrie added that they were asking for information on a black beanie found in the upper Gardens. "It's an Adidas beanie, embroidered with the silver fern. It may or may not have something to do with the investigation, but if you have any information please call the 0800 BOTANIC phone number."

'In other news, protestors in Washington—'

Gary turns off the engine, gets out of his car and sets the keys on top of the driver's tyre. Having been home, having been so close to home and bed, he couldn't face lonely Opoho, so after Dundas Street he'd driven back to Belleknowes and spent the night parked around the road from his old house.

Ducked low in the driver's seat, he'd watched Melanie pass. Following far enough to know she'd park up by the reservoir, he then went back down to George Street and up the Leith Valley to this below-the-reservoir entry-point. His plan is to bump into her on the track, or, if that doesn't happen, to say he was jogging when he saw Kelly's car and thought to wait for her there.

So now he's walking with people's fenced homes on each side—there's no birdsong, just a rhythmic ticking from the power lines. Soon, though, it's all native bush, and the track forks left to a bridge that gets you onto a path that squiggles past a tiny, historic explosives shed, past tall walls of rock that were part of the Woodhaugh Quarry, and down to where Ross Creek becomes Leith Stream, or right to the reserve's main path. That's where Gary goes, with the creek on one side and on the other beech trees entangled in vines, tree stumps decorated with burnt-orange fungus and head-sized, sharp-edged rocks fallen from more of the quarry's thirty-metre walls.

On field trips (before bulk-funding, Gary used to bring both history and geography pupils here) or doing duty, or during normal period-time, one thing a teacher should always be alert to is students whose personal hygiene suddenly nose-dives. Body odour, dirty hair, uniform issues—all are likely to indicate depression, anxiety, and/or stress at home. A chaotic internal life leads to behavioural problems. So, with Melanie's reaction to his appearance in mind, before the track steepens, Gary finds a place to scramble down to the creek, where he squats, scoops water onto his face and starts to wash his neck, head and hands.

Melanie's laugh is famous: a wet, warbling sound that, with the right joke, can go on and on. It's what he's hungry for. Alone all night in the car it's what he realised meeting her this morning had to be about. He'll tell her he loves her—there are plenty in his generation who never say it, but not him. He'll talk about them getting into some running—*Look at you! Out so early!*—and then he'll try her with a joke or two.

Dripping but clean—now at least she won't mistake him for some early-morning madman—and using exposed tree roots that are black as snakes, Gary pulls himself back onto the track, takes aim at the reservoir and, for the first time in years, starts jogging.

The start of Lap Three and still no other cars in the car park. Melanie checks her time—16:01. Right. Do the last two laps in less ten minutes and she gets her PB.

'Then let's go, let's go,' she half says, half thinks, then spits, wipes driblets of spit from her chin, and reaches further with her stride, using her arms to increase her speed while not moving her head, as if it's a bowl of soup her neck's carrying.

Past the small, sloping, grassed area. Past the tree someone has sprayed with 'Fuck Donald Trunk'.

Still no other runners.

Against the energy her brain is putting into proper form, into absorbing the noise and faint sinking sensation of running the gravel, against the different patterns of green the bush makes, past that alarmed thrush fluttering hard to find its wing, comes the word EERIE.

Scared people must be at home on their treadmills. Their spin-cycles. Here it's just her, her and three paradise ducks getting into something on the reservoir. If the Gardens are closed wouldn't you expect an overflow here? Like when the St Clair pool closes for the summer, clogging Moana's lanes?

But that thinking doesn't hold long. Because, nearing the water tower, the increased stress she's putting her body under sets lights flashing on her dashboard: a little catch in her breathing, a slight wobbling of that bowl of soup, less rhythm in her elbows. Lactic acid is beginning the process of shutting her physiology down—how glorious!—and her mind clears, allowing just one final, two-part, thought: if the sex fiend has migrated to Ross Creek how would he catch her? And if he did somehow catch her, she'd take him by the ankles and swing him head first into a tree. Because *she* is thunder, *she's* the killer, and when her machine tells her it's weakening, she says go faster, and so, reaching into the deep parts of her musculature—more speed, more power—she presses turbo, starting a different, noisier breathing, and letting her face fall from 'Mrs Relaxed Focus' to 'Ms Insane Rage' as she tornados into the bend, gravel firing like a shotgun's blast from her sky-blue shoes.

In the way of ice coming away from a great shelf, pride breaks off Gary's heart. Look at her—holy shit!—his little girl. Whoosh! Flying! Here and then gone! Behind the tree he swivels, watching her go, close—dangerously close?—to where the unfenced track drops away.

His daughter the gazelle—or something on a runway, something very near take-off. Wanting to applaud, wanting to roar in approval, he instead grips the tree. Remember when she was eighteen months? Walking with zombie arms, endlessly tripping over those little gumboots, pigtails tied with pink-and-white scrunchies, giggling, always giggling—what did Kelly say that time? *Our daughter's laugh sounds of the most beautiful rain.*

Kelly was right. Why not admit it? She's been right a lot over the years. And really, it's not like any of this is surprising. When Melanie was eight and they'd jog around the block after dinner she'd set the timer on his Casio to seven minutes, leaving the watch in the mailbox—the idea being to get home before the beeping started.

Ducks call on the reservoir. He comes away from the tree and steps onto the track. It's steep all right, down to this concrete trench. He walks up a bit and back. Will she come around again? Or should he set out after her? If she does come, should he jump out waving his arms and making a ghost sound? Melanie's always loved horrors and this is the perfect setting. The cool grey quiet, the bush crowding in.

Gary drops into a hamstring stretch. We just need a monster, some lonely, disturbed creep with advanced skills in the violent arts. But in what sort of horror movie does the young woman easily outrun the monster? Though Gary doesn't feel like a total slug—jogging up to the reservoir he felt quite strong. And maybe she wasn't going *that* fast, maybe it was the fancy running clothes and the short hair, maybe it was the shock of seeing someone moving so well, and *then* realising that that person was your daughter.

He stands straight and in his classroom voice—as if it's the capital of Switzerland he's asking for—says, 'What sort of father can't get into fifth gear for his daughter?'

A thrush comes out onto the track as if it's going to answer 'Bern, sir', then hops to the edge of the trench, looks one way, then the other, and flies off.

'Come on, Mel,' says Gary, listening for her back down the track.

There's the joking he wants to do, there's the discussion he wants to have about his online thing, and now, what also seems important is:

'Since your birth, when faced with a decision, the question I've always kept in mind is, what's best for you. What's best for Melanie? Giving up smoking, say. Well, that was easy. There's the secondhand smoke to consider, and there was my health as your dad, so despite the pleasure Rothmans gave me, I quit. Same as sticking at it with your mum. I've seen enough failed marriages torpedo young people's chances to know that me and Kelly staying together this long will pay dividends later in your life.'

Or something like that. Maybe it's best not to mention Kelly. Really, this meeting, this conversation, needs to be about him and Melanie.

He starts walking in the direction she ran. If she's coming around again, she'll pass him. If not, he needs to be at her car, waiting.

Meeting sex fiend after Lap Five. That would be bad. At least for a few minutes, while she's puking or whatever, any old man could come and drag her into the bush. By the end of Lap Five she'll be lying on the track like a baby, but anyway, here's the car park and what's her time? 20:59. On track. Just keep this pace. This pace. This pace. Sharp there for a moment, her mind again goes vague with the pain happening. She registers a blackbird, Donald Trunk, those paradise ducks, a faint darkening in the light. The toes of blue shoes flash below her eyes. Next is the water tower.

Maximal heart rate equals 220 minus your age. *Lactate produced during extreme exertion results in the burning sensation often felt in active muscles.* Every part of her is under strain—the sensation is of running *through* her skin, of bursting it apart with bone and muscle, of leaving a pale skin-puddle behind her on the gravel. The water tower, the bend after the water tower. Something wet happens around her face—a sneeze? Did she cough out some puke? Did a bird shit on her? It doesn't matter, doesn't doesn't matter matter. Pin down form—hold head on neck and neck on shoulders. Goodbye, bend. Hello, back straight. Come on pain, come right on in.

Smoking's just another human urge. Gary talked about it with the young woman last night, pointing to the dangers on his fingers: heart disease, cancer, emphysema.

Shadowed, her small face was indistinct, as if drawn on a balloon that had then deflated. 'You're smoking tailor-mades,' Gary said. 'I started the giving-up process by switching to roll-your-owns. Over time, it's a good way to thin down usage.'

As though she'd just figured out what he was talking about, she looked hard at the cigarette. 'Right,' she said, drawing out the word, sounding more than a little spacey.

By then he'd been on the footpath, standing by the passenger door, and here he'd opened the door, across the footpath. So that standing the way he was it would have only taken a raised arm to block her path—like one of those farmers on *A Dog's Show* with the crook, the open gate, and that intense, hopeful expression as the sheep decided whether to bolt or follow into the pen.

That was last night's position. Now he's waiting on a narrow part of the track by the edge of the trench, just on from a little bend so she won't see him until she's quite close, so that rather than giving her a fright, he'll just be a nice surprise. Waiting because he's heard her, she's coming.

'Huffing and puffing, like a freight train,' he says, jogging on the spot for a few steps and then going deep into a groin stretch.

'Sexual intercourse is another urge.'

'What?'

'To understand your particular urge, isolate it by clearing the dead wood.'

Blinking, the girl's lids looked heavy as a tuatara's, but now there was a sharpness to her speech. '*Dead wood*?'

'Some people smoke when they're nervous.'

'I'm not nervous.'

He's going to run *with* Melanie. There is that list to get through with her, but sometimes, with younger people especially, actions speak loudest. Join some of the tougher boys for a game of touch at lunchtime and without sharing even a word you'll find your after-lunch lesson on the New Zealand Wars goes much more smoothly. Sharing intense physical activity brings humans together.

'Look at army boot camps,' goes Gary, talking loud, because, now that *they're* almost together, he's nervous.

He hasn't seen Melanie since that day in the lounge, since she looked like she wanted to whack him. But it will be okay, they'll run—he comes up out of his groin stretch—they'll share a little suffering and then:

1. Make her laugh.

2. Explain the computer stuff.

3. Let her in on the motivation behind his decision-making process.

She's close now—hear her breath, hear the sound of her shoes on the path. Obviously, it's some lap-based timed thing she's doing. He jogs a few steps down the track, stops, and jogs back.

Last night's joke—talking to the young lady—was, 'If I raised my arm, just like this, I'd be blocking the footpath.'

23:08. Her blue feet flash. The motion of her arms is more like a swimmer's. And, and, the need to get air, the need to breathe—that urge, it's sort of stuck in her throat, like it's part of what's making it hard to breathe. It's running she's doing, she knows that. She knows her name. Mostly her brain is light—light from a bomb, not a bulb. But just a little further and she can stop. She knows that too. Her arms, her legs, her lungs. If it wasn't for the trench, if it wasn't for that thing ahead in the middle of the track, maybe she'd close her eyes.

Here she is. Not looking so good this time—as though she's being dragged behind some fast thing. Too late, really, Gary realises the section of track he's chosen is too narrow. Either she'll have to stop—she doesn't look like stopping!—or he'll have to run quite a long way to where the track widens. Because what he had in mind was her running up beside him running. Then, glancing at her, he'd say, ultra-casual, 'Fancy seeing you here.'

Corny, but sometimes the best jokes are. And what he then figured was that they'd stop and he'd look at her, his beautiful girl, and he'd start crying. It would be a good way into the computer thing—but it won't just serve a purpose. He's her dad—above everything else, he loves her.

Dad?

'Melanie?'

Closing on him she's become almost unrecognisable—as though the speed of her running has wiped something off her face and for a moment he wonders if he's been watching the wrong girl. But then, in a flash, standing there like a relay runner, skipping down the track a little but also watching back, he sees it definitely is Melanie, and in recognising her, in having her approach in this way, what comes over Gary is terror. He is prey. She is predator. There's nothing to do but run.

Meat Pack

Tom's got croup. Between bouts of coughing—a seal's barking—his tiny two-year-old body is laundry against my chest. Alan's asleep in the next room. I'm on the bed, my back against the wall, and here's Tom. Mouse-smelling hair, a urine tang from his nappy. The in-breath has been hard—snaring in his throat—but now, falling towards sleep, it smooths out.

'*Mummy*,' he says, whispering.

It's worst when he's upset, so I keep my voice gentle as a lullaby. 'It's okay, mate—you're okay.'

'*Mum*.'

'Mum's in Invercargill,' I say, and then with the outside of my thumb I stroke the soft curve of his cheek and he settles further. I pull up the duvet. I've tried Ibuprofen and Panadol and sleeping him on two pillows. I gave him water. I turned up the heat-pump. Nothing's helped. Alan had it, but never this bad. I know what Ann will say if I ring. *Drive them both to the ED. It's the wheezing not the coughing I'm worried about*. But it's cold and late and the ED will be scary: blood, drunks and screaming.

Beside the bed the owl-shaped humidifier sends up two jets. A beat later, Tom's arm rises, saluting, and then falls. 2:13 reads the alarm clock's squared red digits. If his breathing is still not right by 3:00 I'll take them. My gut's a cold revolving globe. I *lack* in these situations. Not assertive. Not brave. As much as I'm worried about Tom, I worry that venturing out in an uncontrolled state will put me in a situation that will expose my cowardice to the world. I count a long breath in and tip my pelvis, trying to release a lumbar twinge. More than twenty years I've had this buggered back. All the weight training when I was young—all the physically demanding jobs I used to do.

Tom shifts, straining a little like he's going to start again, but then just settles higher on the ladder of my body. My hands span his torso as warm wings.

'Shh, my love,' I say.

Delicately I shift my pelvis. Then I tilt my head back so my bald spot's against the cool wall.

That day in 1997 on the North Shore with Phil and Dave, that's when I first hurt my back.

We'd gone offsite to do a job Phil had arranged on the sly. I didn't know Auckland then, but now, thinking on it, we drove to one of the East Coast bays. Not that that matters; what made an impact was Phil, our foreman, backing a timber laden trailer up this steep snaky driveway.

Doing reconnaissance, we'd parked on the bush-lined road—flowering pōhutukawa—and walked up the drive. Narrow, blind in places, freshly planted on each side with clusters of ferns.

In deference, me and Dave walked a bit behind Phil and I remember Dave getting my attention with a doubtful noise and then gesturing at a particularly gnarly section.

'No way, bro,' he whispered.

A cattleman's hat, khaki shorts belted around his narrow waist, Phil had made a fortune building swimming pools in Sydney then lost everything on a downswing. Outraged nostrils permanently shaped by his business failures, he'd clap his hands like a schoolteacher when he was pissed off and give you 'Fucker, useless motherfucking arsehole' sort of stuff until the heat went and he'd trudge back to his office in the little portable container thing at the front of the building site.

Anyway, once we'd seen the driveway become the house we returned to the van where Phil put on his sunglasses and got the vehicle into position. Dave asked if he should stay outside and help navigate, but Phil waved him away. Now, in the back, we went quiet, like it was a tennis game we were at and the top seed was about to serve, the top seed being Phil who rolled his window down to adjust the side mirror. I remember a dense cicada sound—it must have been high summer—and Phil in those sunglasses. With little leather sleeves beside each lens he resembled a hunting bird. He revved the van lightly, the way a rider might whisper into the ear of a horse about to be asked for tremendous speed, and then, sitting still and calm, his freckled fingers light on the wheel, he slid the van into gear and reversed all the way up the drive, without slowing, without the addition of any sense of danger either, just smoothly, like we were ribbon unfurling in an upwards direction, like the trailer had an engine and it was the thing doing the towing.

*

Tom comes off my chest like an adder, coughing hard into my face. His eyes slants, his mouth a hole in the night-light's half dark. Tense, gaping like a nestling, the life of him all focused in chest and throat.

'Mate,' I say. 'Mate.' And then, because Dave's been right there in my ear, 'You're okay, bro. It's okay.'

But again, and again he coughs, some sort of machine failing to start.

It's 2:40.

'Shh,' I say, trying the thing with my thumb again.

Inhaling's hard, like he's having to work up enough wind to force a trap door in his throat.

'Shh, love, shh,' I say.

But it gets worse.

'Shit.'

Getting him to one side, I climb out of bed and pick him up.

And in standing, what comes to me is taking Alan outside when he had croup—looking for Moon, we used to call it. Didn't Ann say croup was inflamed breathing tubes? Then cold air makes sense—you ice damaged muscles to bring down swelling.

Doors at the end of the bedroom open onto a deck and then the land runs to bush and a stream bed where Alan and I set possum traps and so out we go, into the cold and dark.

Looking around, Tom stops coughing.

'Stars,' I say.

Tom came down here with me and Alan once and has never forgotten the dead animal's ugly pink snout, its curved claws.

'*Bed*,' he says, pulling at my face.

I turn out of reach. 'Wonder if there's a moon?'

'*Sleep*,' he says, which just means he wants to go back inside.

'Is there a moon?' I say, emphasising my interest. 'Is te marama up?'

He coughs into my throat, but not for so long.

There's an old mattress in Alan's room we use for jumping games. If I found that blue-and-orange sleeping bag, could we sleep out here?

'*Mummy*.'

'Mum's in Invercargill,' I sing.

The deck is cold under my feet. I'm shivering. But he's inhaling better and some of the tension's gone from the muscles between his ribs.

'Thirty more seconds, bro.'

By thirty he's stopped coughing and is hard against my chest. Wind gusts down through the bare limbs of a kōwhai and I go back into the bedroom. Whatever the physiology, going outside seems to have worked. Tom's breathing is more even. It's 2:47—if he can just sleep for the next three hours. I lay him high up on two pillows and put my back to him, shifting my cold feet one over the other.

The house, that summer day, it was owned by an Italian restaurateur. The timber was to put down boxing for a concrete path.

'Ciao, ciao Phil!'

We got out of the van and looked. From an upstairs window he raised a glass of something. He looked drunk. Dave and I were already unloading the trailer when he came down. Smoking, Phil had stayed in the driver's seat. Dressed in an expensive-looking tracksuit, the restaurateur hugged him through the window. And then, indiscreetly, though Phil's movements gave just as much away, he handed Phil a wad of folded notes.

I remember the driveway and the way that money changed from one man's hand to the other and I remember Dave and me being in good spirits—it was a Friday, for a start, and it was good to be free from the building site. We unloaded, took instructions from Phil, who then left, and started in on the boxing. At 5:30 the Italian came with beer, inviting us to drink it in his carport.

'Or, hey,' he said with his accent, 'wherever you like, no?' making a gesture, as if the North Shore was ours, as if we, as kings of the area, could decide exactly where we'd enjoy that six-pack of DB Export.

But neither Dave nor I were kings of anything. He'd been sergeant at arms in Black Power. He rented in Northcote. His wife did nights at a massage parlour in Takapuna, so Dave usually slept on his couch. He only talked about her once. She was in Rotorua, working. When she got back, and to celebrate her birthday, they'd take LSD and go to Valentines. Sometimes he teased her by saying she wasn't that good, that he was surprised anyone, even Rotorua losers, were paying for it.

Dave had something wrong with his eyes—some days they'd be red and weepy—and he had glue ear. There'd be pus out his ear, down his neck. No doubt some or all of that contributed to his temper. It was worse than Phil's, the difference being that within Dave's anger was the real threat of violence. He'd throw down his tool belt and hold his body not with his hands raised to punch but in the frame just before that. Tense, tipped forward, his feet a wide base. An Irish dad, a Māori mum, tattoos, a sparse moustache, jeans every day no matter the temperature, he smoked Holidays and drove an unwarranted, unregistered, seat-belt free Cortina. He looked like someone from *Crimewatch*, like one of the bad guys in *Once Were Warriors*, though my mate would have made tomato sauce out of Dr Ropata, squeezing him across the pies he ate every morning smoko.

To me he was kind, friendly from my first day. I'd never worked on a building site and he always helped if one of the other builders tasked me with something beyond my skill level. Use a grinder to cut back some reinforced steel, erect a scaffold, measure and cut dwangs with a drop saw. I'd ask Dave and patiently he'd show me how, lending me gloves or goggles, telling me a joke, giving me a cigarette.

'And no rush, bro, there's no rush—them cunts can wait,' he'd say, gesturing at the rest of the building site.

The working with power tools, the ear thing, he was a bit deaf. And maybe he figured what he had to say wasn't important, so he mumbled into the choker chain he wore around his neck. Add in all the swearing and you might have thought Dave spoke a different language.

If I couldn't figure out what he'd said I'd just nod and laugh and raise my eyebrows. But mostly we were silent.

Sat, during smoko, on a concrete pad, down with the wood shavings, the colourful clippings of electrical wire, the thin strips of metal the timber from the yards came belted in.

We did have one running joke. I'd offer him scroggin—brought from my flat in an old Molenberg bag—and he'd look, squinting at the sultanas, dark chocolate, and peanuts shedding their tan skins.

'What? Nah. Food for your rabbit, bro!'

But then he'd eat, tossing his head back, smacking his lips as if what I'd given him was better than anything.

2:57. I roll back to Tom. Asleep. Ann's long lashes. High fat cheeks, a dimpled chin no one can explain. Has his breathing shallowed? What's with his colour? Is it just the way the night-light casts shadows? Out of bed, I cross to the light, turn it on, and come back close. Under their lids his eyeballs wobble at the brightness, but he sleeps on. He's pale. No doubt he's pale. But with a virus running that's expected. What you don't want to see is darkening around the mouth.

2:59. Purring and then roaring for a moment the heat pump comes on and then, satisfied it's found its level, it stops just as suddenly. I go back and turn the light off. Is Tom okay? Or am I too scared to really check? Isn't it best if he's asleep? The responsibility. Jesus. What if I had a heart attack? What if I stroked out and was half dead when the kids woke? What would they do? Alan might be able to get something to eat, but it's hard to see him helping Tom. Piss dragging down their nappies, the freezing house . . . What they'd do is cry and scream and beat me with their fists until their hearts or brains gave out.

I lie down. My own heart's wobbled south so it's now beating up against that cold orb of worry. I breathe into it, trying to calm with oxygen. Redirect brain direction. Ann, Invercargill, Takapuna: I'll google Dave in the morning. We'll all be up and okay and it will still be dark and the penguins can have their Weet-Bix in front of TV, while, with hot, sweet coffee, I'll google Dave, Phil, the Poenamo Hotel, because after that beer at the Italian's, that's where we went. The Po. I'd always said I couldn't when Dave invited me—outside the building site he was from a different world, one I was afraid of. But after three fast beers it seemed like an idea.

'Just a jug,' Dave had said. 'Fucking Friday, bro. *Friday*.'

There was a lounge bar, a TAB/bottle store, and then the public bar. It was busy, but we took one of the tall tables in the middle of the place and Dave went and got jugs and glasses. He poured, we sculled, he poured again. We smoked and kept at the drinking. There were other tradesmen at other tables and some tables of women. Everyone doing pretty much the same as us. The Exponents, Split Enz. I couldn't hear anything Dave said. He was talking a lot though and laughing into his beer, lighting one cigarette off another. I leaned into the table. I smiled. Dave said something about Phil and made a jerking off motion with his hand. Quickly the cold beer filled me with a good feeling.

A raffle happened. Two dollars a ticket. Fifty tickets. The winner got the pot. Dave bought twenty-five tickets and won. Two women from the table nearest ours came over. Dave went to the bar for his prize and came back with jugs—three in one hand, two in the other. Late afternoon sun speared into the pub, sparking in the glassware and the beer. Dave Dobbyn came on the jukebox and the place roared like a bushfire. Froth in his moustache, Dave drank deeply from a jug. Seeing me watching, he set his arm across my shoulders. 'Bro.'

His arm was heavy as a ship's chain, so when noise swelled somewhere and he swivelled I shifted beneath his weight. Repositioned, I dipped my face into a jug. Beer dripped from my chin. An ashtray smoked with unstubbed butts and high on my outer thigh was a hand. Her back to me, one of the women was reaching as if for a relay baton. Long unpainted fingernails, cropped hair, a raggedy collar around the neck of her T-shirt. While I looked, she squeezed. Shifted her hand, then squeezed again. The backs of her ears were tattooed deep green, earrings flashing like lures.

'Going to piss, bro,' I shouted, collapsing out from under Dave.

For a moment the woman's hand stayed mid-air then it fell, and I turned, aiming at a door I'd seen other men come and go from.

From birth I'd been released only into safe zones. School, Moana Pool, the movies, friends' houses. University was more of the same. Flatting, attending lectures, flocking to the pub with others from the same background. But the building site was a new plane. Like TV prison, where hard-bitten inmates endlessly monitor for signs of weakness.

Can he carry that big sheet of Gib? Can he swear so much his sentences lose meaning? Is he unmoved by cold/heat/hunger?

One time a sub-contractor in a Portaloo burped so loudly the green plastic door vibrated. Credit earned. Points, similarly, were handed out for facial hair, drink-driving and rooting. Failure meant bullying. Failure meant becoming the antelope falling back from the herd, while the other antelopes became lions. Rejoining the herd meant fighting, or at least showing willingness.

'Wanna go, cunt?'

Week nights I'd lift at a gym in Newton, so I was strong enough for the Gib. Weekends had always equalled booze and weed so I could hold my own there. But violence and the threat of violence terrified me. Dave's rages, even Phil's half-cooked stuff—I still remember it, the shapes of their faces, the noise, as with Dave, of anger bunching and gathering momentum. I was a coward—that explained my hyper-awareness—and what terrified me most was being called out in front of other men.

Another significant segment of my character was horniness. Women. Once they got to know me, they'd find me so mysterious, so in touch. Wow! I imagined them saying, strong *and* sensitive! Listen to the insight he has about his parents' divorce, about his binge-drinking degree from Otago University, about the personalities at his job. He *understands* himself, he *thinks.* They'd be taking off their knickers and queuing up as if I was a ride at an amusement park.

Though reality had me nowhere near any of that. Zero

sex experience and less than zero confidence. When a woman put her hand on my thigh, what did I do? Scuttled. Not that I let my weak self show as I crossed that pub—past painters, sparkies and dusty Gib stoppers—keeping my chest out and my face free of expression.

But what sort of man can't fuck or fight?

And maybe it was correlating those character traits that did it, or maybe it was the beer, the music, and being mates with the toughest man in Auckland, or it could have been the construction site—violence must have been growing in me the same way weights had grown my fingers that were now broad as breakfast sausages—but whatever the reason, crossing a narrow section of lino, through a heavy door into what I thought were the toilets, I, for the first time, experienced a violent urge, an urge built on hate for my pathetic inner self, and hate for the outer world—for the way it amplified what a wimp I was.

The outer world which in this case wasn't urinals or sinks but a man, a man looking up at one of four televisions. Horse racing. Not a place to piss, but the TAB part of the pub. The man was Phil.

The big door sucked shut, quietening the noise. Head tilted at where horses were finding their way into the stalls, Phil slid his eyes over me. 'That boxing done?'

In just the same fuckwit tone he'd use to order me around the building site. The time, laughing with one of the hardware reps, he got me to waterblast the Portaloo's interior. The time he asked if everyone who rode the city's buses was a poofter.

Cars passed on the road in front of the pub. The betting

counter was vacant. Anger boiled, but I had no experience in its expression.

'Had a few then?' he sneered, responding to my mute state. When I didn't answer, he nodded in the direction of the pub. 'You with the whore's husband?'

Back then, picking shit up was my life. Weights, timber, sacks of concrete mix. So that's what I did. Picked Phil up. I went in low, looped my right arm around his knees and scooped him so my face was level with his groin. When I drew my arm back he came level with my waist and I wrapped my left arm around his chest so that I had him horizontally, the way I carried the scaffolders' long planks.

He didn't like it, bashing with his arms, kneeing my kidneys. But he was short and thin and, having acted, my anger had burnt down to fear. What would he do if I let him go? So I held tight—crushing him against my side like a basket of laundry I was terrified of dropping. Then there was sound at the counter and suddenly embarrassed to be doing this in private I aimed at the door I'd just used, opening it with a kick, and as if Phil was a gun I was going to rob the place with I went back into the pub. For a moment no one noticed—the place still roared—then some concrete-cutters looked.

'Meat pack, meat raffle,' said one in a normal voice, nodding at me and Phil and elbowing his plus-sized mate who, in a louder, auctioneer's voice, said, 'Meat raffle! Meat pack!'

Tables stood and turned. People raised jugs. The place was a sea of teeth and beer-wet gums. And the chant caught on. 'Meat pack! Meat pack! Meat pack!'

Hands hammered tables, work boots stamped, drowning whatever the jukebox was doing. Some would have worked for Phil—'Phil, ya cunt!'—but others could tell by his age and wardrobe that he was one of the types always telling them what to do, how to do it, and how long the delay would be before they were paid.

A mob behind me—*me!* Wanting them kept, I bent my back and muscled Phil into a different position, raising him by his belt, getting him onto my shoulder, tipping him forward, turning him into some huge foetus I was selling. People pressed close, beer spilled. Phil kicked his heel, tomatoing my nose. 'Chuck him!' someone shouted. 'Chuck the fucker!'

3:29. I turn back to Tom. Head tipped to one side, his breath has smoothed. His philtrum's tiny scoop. Hair curling beneath the ragged edges of his ears.

How my boys would be stunned to see me with a man perched on my shoulder! To see me squatting a little, rotating, and sending him sailing out over the crowd. Not that that part ever happened. Before it could, Dave was there, in as tight as a dance partner, taking Phil as though he was fruit and I was some arsehole tree. He didn't unrumple Phil's shirt or anything, just got him down, glanced at me and then went back to our table, to where it was we'd been having such a hot time.

I remember Phil putting his hand to his head, as though wondering if a hat he'd been wearing was still in place. I remember sweat breaking over my whole body.

The crowd sagged back. People sneered. 'Pussy,'

someone said. 'Faggot.'

At least I didn't run. I remember ducking, though, as if suddenly the tavern's roof had lowered, and rather than leaving a pub I was descending steep stairs into some dark cellar. Out of the pub—a long blue handrail, a gravelled car park—across the road, onto the hard turf of the league fields there, running by then, running past two boys practising up-and-unders, running past two boys swearing in the pleasure of the bombs they were making.

Alan sweats like me. No matter how we prepare him for sleep his hair makes wet forks against his forehead, the rest of his mop a wire cloud hanging back from his face. Skin like milk. And Ann. Asleep in some motel. Her phone there by her hand. One knee resting on the other, the splendid curve of her hip. I roll back onto my side, but rise again to sip from the glass on the bedside table.

That night—after the Po—I experienced my first dose of back pain, around my belt-line, down the back of my right leg. The next day I went around my flat crouched like a crab. Twenty years ago—twenty!—and as strong as I'll ever be. Probably as scared, too. Strong, drunk, scared. These days, with my back the way it is, there's no helicopters for the boys. No tossing them up against the sun.

I rest my head on the pillow, following its curve down to the clock.

I still can't back a trailer. Or use a nail gun. I can only imagine handling a machine powerful enough to cut concrete. I never saw Dave again. I never saw Phil. I'm just here with Tom and Alan. Passing on what I am to them.

Stone vs Cog and Rabbits

With the tide right out the three boys made their first rectangle on the flat, hard sand, near the waterline.

'Wider,' said Stone.

'We're playing seven rounds,' said Cog.

Rabbits looked at where Cog was on the beach. 'Yeah, wider,' he said.

Cog shrugged and went further away from the water with his bike helmet.

Four corners. Two helmets because Cog and Rabbits had ridden from Belmont, and two corner flags—Stone's dad had got them for him—that were as tall as the ones used in the holes at the golf course.

The field marked, the boys came together near halfway, Stone spinning the white Adidas from one hand to the other.

'Perfect conditions, mate,' went Rabbits, with an Australian sports commentator's twang.

'Not much of a crowd,' followed Cog.

Most of the people on the beach were joggers or dog-walkers. Out towards Rangitoto, heading for the channel, a man in jeans waded the shallows with a surfcaster. Up the beach, near the big pōhutukawa and the outdoor shower, a man and woman were settling on the sand.

'C'mon then, fuckers,' said Stone.

Stone whose house was just there—big, fancy, spaceship grey—with first its low wire fence and sign that said 'Security Sensors Operating' and next with this broad, close-cut lawn where little robot-type sprinklers were already showering water around the place.

'Whose kick-off?' said Rabbits.

He and Cog were neighbours, them and their mums taking up the first two of a three-unit brick set-up just back from the Belmont shops.

'Mine,' said Stone.

With him bigger and a year ahead of them at high school, the way they always played was Stone vs Cog and Rabbits.

Cog and Rabbits who now backed away from halfway, spreading out. Cog acted casual about beach rugby—like it was cool and that, but also like there were other places it would be equally cool to be. Really, though, he'd slept in his board shorts, crying in frustration late last night when their shitty internet had failed, leaving him unable to double-check the tides and forecast.

'Watch the short one,' he now said, as Stone feinted to drop short, but then hoisted a high up-and-under towards Rabbits.

Rabbits was tall and skinny—underfed, Cog's mum said—but he was a brave fucker, and he went high and made the catch, landing as Stone arrived and tackled him back onto the sand.

'One,' said Stone, standing, cutting his eyes at Cog.

They called it beach rugby, but it was closer to league. Five tackles and then the kick. No line outs—the other team/player just got the ball—and no scrums. Again, just a handover. For Cog and Rabbits the tackled player had to tap and then pass, and that's what Rabbits did now to Cog who went straight at Stone.

Stone who was in a singlet and Sonny Bill haircut, Stone who grabbed Cog ball-and-all, swivelled and took him off his feet, slamming him onto the beach.

'Two,' said Cog, getting up just as fast as Stone, tapping the ball with the inside of his foot and spiralling wide to Rabbits.

At maybe seven metres this would be their widest field. As they tired, they shrank the field's width, but it was only ever five tries to win. Skill did come into it—especially the end-of-set grubbers and the passing/offloading between Cog and Rabbits—but mostly it was about the collisions. That was why they were there, that was what they liked.

'Three,' said Cog.

Taking the pass, Rabbits had swerved for the sideline, making Stone dive around his ankles.

'Out,' said Stone, getting up.

Rabbits stayed down, looking. 'Cog?' he said.

Cog went over and checked down the sideline towards a helmet, then at Rabbits and the divots his body had made in the sand. 'Nah,' he said. 'Not out.'

What Cog said in these situations was law. For some reason, on beach rugby days he was the boss. Not at school, fuck no, there Stone was as far from him and Rabbits as you could get. Stone with his fades and good clothes, with his name always up at assembly for the rep-teams he'd made.

Tackle four and Cog took the pass from Rabbits, slowed, and then burst forward, hard into Stone, raising his ball-carrying arm high, trying to drop the ball off to Rabbits who saw the move coming and went fast off Cog's right shoulder, but though Cog got the ball free their timing was just off, or maybe Stone did enough with the tackle. Anyway the ball landed on the sand as Stone lifted one of Cog's legs and drove him back.

'Fucker,' said Cog as Stone let him go.

It was the word the boys around school were using most.

Dribbling the ball with his feet, Stone went back past Cog, holding his hand hip-height for Cog to slap. Like he'd seen All Blacks do after a mistake, Cog put his hands on his hips, looked up at the blue sky, turned slowly, and spat. Rabbits was bent, looking at something in the sand, then he stood and skimmed a white shell into the shallows. Out by the channel, the man was casting.

'Trying for kingies,' said Stone, in a way that suggested he knew all about fish and fishing.

Rabbits came back, indicating *Next time, bro* by also slapping Cog's hand.

'Sashimi, boy. That's the way to eat 'em,' said Stone, flicking the ball back and up into his hands with his foot.

Rabbits dropped into the crouched, wide-armed position he always adopted on defence. Then he looked over at Cog and winked.

'What?' said Stone.

'Nothing,' said Cog, drying his palms with a handful of sand.

'Don't you know about protein and electrolytes and shit?'

Cog smiled, but didn't say anything. He knew Rabbits would be wearing the same face. They'd been best mates, neighbours and in the same class for so many years that they had this instinctive understanding. Not just at beach rugby, but when they were in class or like now when they were all together and Stone was being this know-all dick.

Stone who now spun the ball in his hands, looking.

He knew about their understanding—you could tell—and you could tell he knew he'd just shown off his other life. But despite his raw-fish lunches and North Shore Under-15s, despite his always hanging at the school's Marble Wall with the other cool kids, their haircuts and headphones, Cog reckoned Stone would have liked to spend lunchtimes with him and Rabbits, playing fives or force-back.

Not that it—the thing between Cog and Rabbits—didn't piss Stone off, and now he tapped, exploding towards the gap between them.

Rabbits went low—unless a try was threatened, he always did—while Cog stayed high, grabbing Stone's fending arm, jumping in front and clattering with him into the sand.

'Nice technique,' sneered Stone, getting up, sniffing and checking his nose for blood.

Cog stayed quiet, just backed away the required metre. Nothing he did was pretty, but usually it worked.

'One,' said Rabbits.

Stone tapped, faked a grubber, and then tried to swerve around Rabbits who went off his feet, wrapping Stone's knees and then ankles, spinning out like a sheet tied behind a bike.

'Two,' said Rabbits, bouncing up off the sand and holding out his arm as if there was a line of defenders and attackers. As if this was AMI Stadium or Eden Park, not just Cheltenham Beach on an already hot teacher-only Thursday.

With his size and strength, Stone usually won most of the early games, but as the day went on, endurance came into it and, if Cog and Rabbits were smart, they could start getting games back. Holding him down in tackles, getting Rabbits running wide. The idea was to drain Stone's muscles and lungs. Between games they always went swimming and Cog would keep at it, encouraging Stone to see how long he could hold his breath and how far he could swim underwater. If Stone wasn't buggered for the later games, with the narrow sidelines, he'd go right over the top of them, and then they'd not only lose but might get hurt.

'Three,' said Stone.

He'd again tried to swerve Rabbits—it was like Stone could never fully accept Rabbits was just as fast as him—who'd again dived and brought him down.

'Raisin's here,' said Rabbits, staying in his low defensive crouch.

Up by Stone's place, a woman was standing in a bikini, and the thing about raw fish and Stone being pissed off with Cog left on the breeze off the Gulf as the boys came together. She was old but with this decent blond hair and a toned, totally tanned body. According to Stone she sunbathed every sunny day in the same spot.

Hoping to get a laugh, Cog waggled his finger, saying in the way of Mr Ross, the vice principal, 'Be sunsmart, men.'

'Her cunt the same colour as the rest of her?' said Rabbits.

Stone laughed through his nose.

'Boys,' said a man in a cap, passing with two little dogs on long leads.

'Morning,' said Stone.

'No school?' said the man, stopping and looking over the top of his sunglasses at Rabbits as if he'd heard the joke and didn't like it.

Girls at school said Rabbits stank. Some called him Pantene as sort of a joke about his long hair. But that didn't stop him being funny or fast. Not that he ever entered the sprints on athletics day or made his jokes around anyone but Stone and Cog—really, Rabbits kept a low profile at school, hardly doing anything that got him noticed.

'Teacher-only day, sir,' went Stone.

He had this arse-licking way with grown-ups, but it worked, and now the man smiled like he'd just helped with something and went away.

'Where were we, ladies?' said Stone.

Maybe Rabbits did smell a bit off at times, plus he had these burn scars on his face that made it look like he'd been mucking around with Sellotape, but shit he could be funny. As much for the way he said things as what he said. If Cog thought about having either one of them as a brother—which he did—he'd choose Rabbits over Stone. Not that it wasn't close.

'Four,' said Rabbits.

'Bullshit. Three,' said Stone.

'Come on, fucker,' said Cog as Stone tapped and went straight at him, holding the ball in one hand.

Not even for cricket were they allowed on Stone's lawn. Not even for tiddlywinks, was how Stone put it. His dad was a big-shot lawyer and Stone joked that Cog saw more of his dad—who was dead—than he did. And at least at Cog's place there were places to sit, and there was a fridge with actual food and drink. At Stone's place—Cog had only been in once—there was all this space. Like burglars had been. And forget getting a drink. 'No way,' Rabbits would say. 'Stone's mum wouldn't let us drink from the toilet.'

Anyway, just as it sometimes felt like Stone lived on a different planet, it sometimes also felt like Stone was playing a different game, like he could score whenever he wanted.

'One nil,' he now said, having gone straight over Cog who, despite having had the lower part of his body strong and stable with his head in a safe place—and therefore his shoulder in the right place—had been steamrollered like he was no more than long grass. Long-Grass-Cog who was now getting more sand to dry his hands, while Rabbits held the ball ready to kick off.

Weirdly, at the northern end of the beach, where the pastel houses were, lots of people—they all looked like women—were sitting listening to a person who, like a ninja, was dressed all in black. Sitting in the shallows the boys had watched the gathering for a bit, and then gone back to comparing the sizes of their feet. From the house next to Stone's came the smell of meat cooking.

Rabbits worked his nose like someone in a cartoon. 'Fucker somewhere barbecuing.'

Heat shimmered. Birds flew in and out of the pōhutukawa. White and high, a helicopter crossed towards the city. Cicadas seed and sawed. If he looked, Cog knew he'd see the different ferries—Kawau, Tiritiri Matangi, Waiheke—working the Gulf. Cog found a pipi in the soft sand. Grabbing it, he held it up and then dropped it back over his shoulder. Up the beach you couldn't tell the woman from the man, they were lying so close. Further along you could make out the hump Raisin made. The tide ate away at the beach. Half the field they'd played that first game on was now harbour.

Stone rolled onto his front, looking out to sea, sipping and then spitting the salty water.

He was ahead two games to nothing. Cog had tried to get him into a swimming race with Rabbits, but Stone wasn't interested. Stone was going to play Super Rugby while at the same time studying to be a doctor. Adults asked all the time, but Cog didn't know. When he was real young he apparently used to say 'Fireman', so that's what he still said. 'A fart surgeon,' Rabbits would say, doing the thing he'd just done with his nose. An *arsehole* cleaner.

Cog copied Stone's move, digging his fingers deep into the soft sand. Their warm shoulders touched for a moment as Cog got settled. Salt dried in the dark stubble of the eyebrows Stone obviously shaped with a razor.

Lately, there'd been rumours Stone had fingered a girl on the Devonport ferry.

'Fisherman's called it a day,' said Stone.

He was coming towards them with his rod, lifting his knees high, splashing water up in front like he was in a hurry.

'Two more games before Stone buys lunch at the bakery,' said Rabbits. He'd stayed facing shore, piling wet sand on the knee he'd raised out of the water.

Wheelbarrowing around, facing up towards the couple, Stone licked surface water. 'Those two up to?'

Cog had turned too. 'Same thing you did with Nina,' he blurted.

Stone looked at him, but didn't speak. Feeling stupid, blushing, Cog wheeled back to watch the fisherman, but Rabbits must have seen because, covering Cog's embarrassment, he crowed, 'Two more games and then I do a big shit in Stone's dad's shower.'

Stone did his nose laugh and then stood, clearing one nostril after the other.

Like with the way he played, you sometimes got the feeling Stone was more adult than kid. More like the student teacher who came and played touch at lunchtime, then went off after school on a motorbike to meet his girlfriend at the Viaduct or Sky City.

Rabbits stood now too, so it was only Cog watching the fisherman. He had a knife on his belt and he was looking right at Cog, not smiling, sort of staring in a way that got Cog looking away and then standing and turning to face in the same direction as his friends.

'Catch anything, bro?' said Stone.

The man turned and smiled, not at Stone but at Cog—he wore one of those hats with the flap down the back—and didn't say anything, just kept kicking through the water.

'Strange-looking fucker,' said Stone, in a voice that was loud and carried. Cog's heart went up, worried the man might have heard, but if he did, he didn't react, just went out of the water, up the beach and past where they'd made a pile of their helmets, corner flags and rugby ball.

'Game three, then,' said Rabbits, following after Stone who was already heading out.

Stone won that one too, the most memorable of his tries coming from a Rieko Ioane–style chip, chase, regather, and dive. With the narrower field the rest were hard grind. Rabbits almost scored, but Cog ruled him held up, and on the next set Rabbits got a bleeding nose bouncing off Stone's shoulder when he and Cog both went high. Stone said that proved Cog's ruling was right, that it was karma, which was something Cog had heard Grant Nesbitt say on Sky once in a similar situation.

Anyway, karma or not, the fact was in three games Cog and Rabbits had scored only two tries, and now, getting ready for the fourth game, Rabbits said what Cog had been thinking. 'If we can't beat him or at least get some tries, he won't want to play with us.'

He had his face up behind the ball, the way Beauden Barrett did when calling a move.

Cog nodded, like it was some special defence formation

they were planning.

'He'll spend all his time on Fullers, fingering Year Tens,' continued Rabbits, which made Cog laugh, causing Stone to stand straight and say, 'C'mon, fuckers.'

The field was now as narrow and long as the corridors at school.

'*C'mon* then, fuckers!' said Rabbits, pirouetting and directing a little up-and-under towards Cog's purple bike helmet, Cog who was already off—it was the way Rabbits had said *C'mon* that let him know the type of kick-off—as Stone closed in too slow and Cog went up AFL-style, like he was trying to catch the sun, and took the ball, landed, cantered across the sand, planted the ball, and then kept on running in a wide arc, over the sand, back through the shallows, past the shells and clumps of rust-coloured weed to where Rabbits held his fist ready for congratulations.

Stone was smiling too and now he did the thing he did with his eyebrows—for him the ultimate sign of respect—and said, 'The new Jeff Wilson.'

Stone watched and talked about the old games as a way—he'd told Cog this straight up—of getting his old man to notice him.

It started a good run for Cog and Rabbits and with some off-loads—a backhanded one from Cog, one around Stone's back, a miracle one from Rabbits—and some luck—'The ball's doing funny things,' Rabbits had shouted—the younger boys won the fourth game.

They were having lunch. Stone had taken Rabbits' bike and ridden to a bakery on Lake Road, coming back with a loaf of bread, some Sprite, two Paddle Pops and a block of Dairy Milk.

Rabbits was burying his ice-cream stick in the sand. He and Cog were on their tummies, drying out having swum in the water that was closer in. Cog burped, stringing chocolatey saliva from his mouth, and then sucked hard, re-mouthing the spit like it was spaghetti.

Stone was sitting looking out at Rangitoto. A breeze was up and, along the beach to the north, three women were unpacking kite-surfing sails. Beyond them, near the pastel-coloured houses built into the rock at the end of the beach, the people—now they were *all* in black—were organising themselves into different formations: long lines like at primary school, a huge circle, something that from above might have looked like a snow flake.

Rabbits moved to get more bread. Wearing Stone's sunglasses, he was hollowing out the loaf and rolling the bread into pills he'd wash back without chewing. Stone yawned, took something from a plastic bag in his pocket and ate it. He'd had some Sprite, but none of the other food he'd bought. The young couple came back. The girl was in a short denim skirt and a singlet. She was tanned, but not crazily. They had ice creams and were laughing as they took off their jandals. Cog watched the girl—the different shapes her body made as she moved—and ground his dick into the sand that was soft and wet from his swim.

'Ready then, fuckers?' went Stone.

Now Cog wanted to piss into the sand, but he didn't think Stone would like it if he did. If Rabbits pissed, Stone would laugh, but that would be because of the way Rabbits handled it, the way he'd chase them with the pine cone of urine-hard sand, and the horrible/hilarious shit he'd say when he did. Cog went back to watching the girl. Then he looked at the seagulls. They had come in when Stone arrived with the food, and still they stood, red-beaked and white. The feeling Cog had was that after the last two games, Stone would leave them. For good. That they'd see him again at school and stuff, but never like this.

Rabbits nudged Cog, who held out his hand thinking he was being offered the Sprite, but the bottle was still on the sand and when Cog looked in the direction Rabbits' nose was pointing it was obvious what had got his attention. The girl, the one with the ice cream, had sat with her legs pointed down this way, and what you could see was this white cotton triangle up top of her brown legs. And then, even better, she laughed and rolled her right leg out a little, showing the creamy skin to the side of her undies.

Air went out of Cog, same with Rabbits, who recovered faster with a wolf's *A ooohhh,* choking a bit at the end of his howl.

The man looked, but the view didn't change, and so Rabbits went again, this time keeping the noise going—high and then higher and then low—for long enough to get even Raisin rising off her towel, her big glasses the windows of a skyscraper, her pale-palmed hand waving—she was lapping it up—and that got Cog giggling, giggling and digging his hard-on into the sand.

As if Cog wasn't giggling and Rabbits wasn't being a wolf, Stone said, 'Well? Are we going to play?'

The worst thing Cog could imagine was Rabbits shifting.

The next worst was Stone ignoring them. That thought stopped him and he had one more look between the girl's legs and then started to get up, but now, like he was giving in to something, Stone rolled, flopped between them, took his sunglasses from Rabbits and grabbed some chocolate.

The couple were still at their ice creams—the view basically unchanged—and when Rabbits drew an arrow in the sand and wrote P U S S Y, Stone must have finally seen because he went, 'Oh, fuuck mate,' in a decent rendition of Rabbits' Aussie commentator thing, and that was it for Cog, who bumped like a dinghy into his mate's shoulder, laughing so hard Sprite leaked out his nose.

Now, in from where the boys had been looking at their feet, the fisherman was swimming. No longer in his T-shirt, still wearing his jeans and his belt with the knife, he was sealing around on his hands, probably getting pipi, but he had no collecting bag, and the feeling Cog had was that he'd gone back out there to watch them. Not that Cog was saying anything—he didn't want to sound scared.

It was three-all now and they'd just measured the last field. It would be like playing in a lift—one of the bigger ones they have at hospital for transporting people in beds—so kicking couldn't come into it. In the case of a seventh game—they weren't common and, as Cog said, it was an occasion to be respected—they played first to seven tries, rather than first to five.

Stone had a cut on his wrist from when he'd gone hard into the sand tackling Rabbits at the end of the sixth game. He was rinsing it down in the water and the man was further out, looking through Stone's legs at Cog, who was reminding Rabbits about not kicking.

'There's no room, we won't risk it.'

'Yeah,' said Rabbits. 'I'll tackle high.'

'And hard, mate.'

Rabbits took him behind the neck and brought his forehead in close so they were touching. On Sky, when the players did it, it looked staunch and sort of aggressive, but here it felt close—more like the hongi they'd sometimes practised back in their primary days.

'We're brick walls,' said Rabbits, bunting Cog lightly.

Cog stepped back, nodding. He was down to his bare chest and the Quicksilver boardies Stone had handed down to him last year. He knew he was skinny—especially his upper half—but still, this was Stone Reihana they were three-all with.

'C'mon, fucker,' he said to Stone's back, this time glaring at the fisherman. But Stone just kept doing whatever he was doing, and the fisherman didn't seem to notice, and trying to stop the confidence squeak out Cog turned and whistled a flat spiral pass into Rabbits' chest.

A towel draped over their middle parts, the couple were back to lying down, and maybe it was the heat moving the air, but it looked like they were vibrating, sort of in time with what the cicadas were still doing. Standing, Raisin waved—she did now, every time she stood and went through some yoga stuff and then changed the place on her body the sun was hitting. Smiling back, like she was an important part of all their lives, letting her know they were all still here and okay, Rabbits held up the ball and waved.

Down the beach the kite-surfers had packed all the gear they didn't need into two shiny saveloy-shaped bags that glowed under the sun. Beyond them, the crowd—they *were* all women—was coming slowly towards them.

'Lady zombies,' said Rabbits.

Coming up the beach, standing beside them, Stone went, 'The fuck?'

'They protesting something?' said Cog.

People were filming with phones. One person on the sea side of the group had a larger camera. There was a helicopter too, but it was high so it was hard to know what it was looking over.

'Protesting what? The summer?' went Rabbits.

They had no placards or whatever and they were dead quiet, so you wouldn't know what it was they wanted to change. And they were getting closer, but only very slowly. It was the way they were walking, raising their feet and then carefully placing them down on the sand like it was a blanket of drawing pins they were on.

'More like an ad for something,' said Stone. 'The Coke guys were here last summer.' Then, as if it was somehow related, 'And this will be my last game, boys.'

Rabbits flicked him the ball. 'Game seven.'

But Stone had said something else, Cog could tell by the way he brought the sweat off his face and plastered down his hair.

'Eh?' said Cog.

Blood from the cut ran down Stone's forearm, forming a drip at his elbow. He looked at Cog. 'Coach doesn't even want us playing casual touch. I got to take care of myself.'

Cog turned, looking for Rabbits who'd backed up as far as the try line, waiting on the kick. Then, just as fast, like something caught in a windstorm, he turned back to Stone. 'This is your last game?'

Stone dropped the ball onto the bridge of his foot, balancing it, and then flicked it back up into his hands. That done, he looked sadly at Cog.

As if in response, one of the kite-surfers cried with pleasure as she took flight, scudding across the water.

Cog turned away. Shitting your pants, having a boner during swimming sports, having a sister who somehow ended up in online porn, even wearing like, a skirt to school, was way better than crying.

Rabbits came up, not touching, but standing close. 'Bro?'

'This is his last game.' Cog looked out again at the man—he was closer in now and still watching them—like it was his fault.

Rabbits nodded as if Stone had told him already. 'Then let's beat him.'

Cog turned back to Stone who glistened like a statue, the only moving part of him the blood dripping to the sand.

Cog sniffed back snot and tried to seem tough by spitting, but it was no good. Tears leaked down his cheeks. And what about Rabbits? Pretty recently, he'd said his mum kept going on about shifting somewhere cheaper, like Waikato or something.

'Ready?' said Stone.

Crouching over so the tears went straight down, Cog got some sand.

With men by themselves—like the fisherman—Cog sometimes imagined they were his dad reincarnated or whatever. He dreamed they'd come up, like in the movies, with a message from the other side: *Hold the line. Be strong in your loyalty.* When what was more likely was the fisherman coming to their unit late at night and raping and killing him or, worse, doing in his mum. And then where would he be?

'Ready?' said Stone again. Not in a hard way, but in a way that said, *Getting this last game going is probably the best thing, bro.*

When Cog had thought that 'hold the line' crap through and tried to use it—for exams, say, or situations like this—he realised it didn't come from Dad, but from the Test Rugby promotions you saw on TV. So what Cog thought of now was his mum telling him how crying was good, how it at least kept your eyes clean and how, really, with his farting, they were probably better off without Dad, and this always got Cog feeling lighter and a bit more aware of whatever it was he was doing, which, right now, was watching the ball Stone held up and out from his body like a waiter with a tray.

Reacting to the blood, or the way the ball was being held, a seagull flew across their game and soared on an updraught, looking with its reptile eye as Stone planted his left foot and kicked an incredible up-and-under, travelling only a few metres forward but going so high it made the bird flicker its left wing casually before swooping towards the city.

At sand level, forgetting everything, Cog stepped back. 'Mine!'

He had to catch this ball. Stone wouldn't let him have it easy like he had that other kick-off. Despite the tears, Stone would do anything to win this last game, and with such a small field first possession would be crucial.

The ball reached the highest point of its trajectory and started to bomb down as, silently, the women in black arrived, surrounding the field like ants around a raindrop, blanking Raisin, the couple and the fisherman, providing the biggest crowd ever, as Cog went forward hard at Rabbits—who'd come in to act as blocker—and leapt, floating his knees.

Stone came on too as Rabbits turtled his head and bowed, facing Stone, and Cog's knees flowed up Rabbits' body, contracting at the highest point, pushing off Rabbits' back the way a gymnast uses the horse, and flying even higher, plucking the ball two-handed—*smack!*—and going over Stone, brushing that neat hair do with his arse, falling hard to the sand, grovelling forward a metre, and planting the ball on the line.

'Try! What a fucking try. Try, fucker! *Try*!'

When they were much older, when it was just Rabbits and Cog left, they talked about it as the time Cog shat on the great Stone Reihana. Later still, when it was just Cog, the way he remembered it, the marchers weren't marchers, they were a flock of blackbirds he was flying with.

What Sort of Man

It was Thursday and on Thursdays Evan looked after Carl. They'd walked at the beach and then the Botanic Gardens. Now they were up Ross Creek, sitting on a wooden seat, looking over the reservoir. It was hot, but the seat was shaded. Two runners went past on the gravel track, disappearing into the bush.

'Runners,' said Evan. 'Enjoying the sun, eh? Keeping fit.'

Carl didn't look. He was busy with a little container of nuts.

Evan was Carl's support worker. They were both in their early thirties.

In front of them, over the water, a kererū went straight up and straight down, trying for the attention of another bird.

'Like a rollercoaster,' said Evan. 'Been on a roller-coaster, Carl?'

Carl looked into the nut container as though it was a microscope. Selecting a nut, he shot a look at his lunchbox which was on the seat between them, made one of his little grunts, and then put the nut in his mouth.

'That's it, mate,' went Evan, quietly. 'That's it, eat those nuts.'

Turning his head away, Carl started breaking up the nut with his teeth.

Carl was non-verbal, but Evan always tried to keep up some conversation. It wasn't easy. Out on the air, when he knew nothing was coming back, his voice sounded strange. Like he'd thought the words, but someone else was using his mouth to say them. Checking he still had the car keys, he took out his phone. He worried about losing them—the keys, the phone—and having some incident/health thing happen with Carl. Though so far, working with Carl, Evan had only needed his phone as a clock. It was almost one, another ninety minutes and then he'd drop Carl back at his flat and drive to South Dunedin to see Bobby, his other Thursday guy.

'Just going to text Jo,' said Evan, like they'd been talking intently, but now he was going to use this silence to do something he'd been meaning to do for a while.

Carl selected another nut.

'Eat those nuts, old man,' went Evan, getting his phone into position to text, 'then you're onto that apple.'

When Carl got worked up—over-stimulated by noise or movement or light, or extra-hungry, or tired, or frustrated because he needed a toilet and you hadn't got him to one—he'd rock, yowl, and pull hair. So on Thursdays Evan wore a cap Jo had got him. The other thing always in Evan's mind was little children. Carl liked shoving them. No one knew why, but he'd done it before. The 'hat' for that problem was staying away from places there were kids and being real alert. Kids moved fast and made loud noises. Their unpredictability—the 'car alarm out of nowhere' aspect of them—was what Evan figured set Carl's nerves on edge.

Checking Carl while writing his text, Evan took off his cap, wiping the sweat from his forehead. *How's bubba? How you? 88 mins to go!*

Evan added a kiss for his wife and then pressed SEND.

'You finished those nuts then, eh? Good man, good man. Have your apple, mate, then we'll go find a toilet.'

Evan spoke in this voice that was halfway between normal and a whisper—the sort of voice you might use to wake someone you loved.

Evan sat back, putting his phone away, and Carl bit into his apple, giving Evan a little fright. After that first shift with Carl, Evan had said to Jo it was like being at war. Boring with lots of waiting and slow walking, but at the same time you knew violence could happen at any moment. Still, it was a month of Thursdays he'd done with Carl and, so far, no problems. But time *did* go slow. Carl wasn't ultra-fit or anything, and anyway it was a five-hour shift, so you couldn't just walk and walk. They could get a coffee or whatever or do things in town like cruise the museum or Meridian Mall, but so far Evan hadn't been game. He was worried about the kid thing, and if Carl was going to pull his hair Evan wanted it to happen somewhere there weren't lots of people to see.

'It's just me and Ed tonight,' said Evan. 'Jo's got this funeral in Ashburton in the morning.'

Carl bit the top off the apple, stalk and all. After a moment he put his finger in his mouth and came out with mulched up woody stuff.

'No thanks, mate. Chuck it away, eh?'

Carl fluttered his hand and the chewed-up stalk went onto the grass in front of them. When they arrived, two ducks had come up from the reservoir to see what was for lunch, and now they came back.

Evan looked at the birds and then took his phone out again. Eighty-six minutes. Carl went back to his apple.

There was more noise on the track and Evan scanned the area of bush where the runners had gone. No doubt he was overly vigilant. It wasn't like Carl was a commando or anything—he couldn't just bounce up and fly after a little child. Still, Evan was a new dad and what he felt, and what he'd told Jo, was that he couldn't imagine anything worse than some stranger hurting Ed.

A dog came down the path and then a smiling older woman with fluoro hand weights. The dog ran towards the seat. Beating hard with their wings, the ducks went off over the reservoir.

'He's friendly, don't worry,' called the woman.

The dog made an arc in the direction the ducks had taken. Evan smiled broadly and waved at the woman. Passing other walkers with Carl, Evan always made an effort to smile and say hello, when if he'd been with Jo the most he might have done was raise his eyebrows. Probably the fact that Carl didn't respond to anyone's greeting made Evan more generous. Also, the violence—or the possibility of it—put Evan on edge, making him more outgoing and eager to have contact, however brief, with other people.

Evan's phone vibrated. He checked Carl—still on the apple—and then opened the message.

All good here. Ed eating banana squish. Already sad about leaving x

Carl made a noise. He was still chewing, but the apple was gone. Evan looked at the phone. Seventy-nine minutes. It would have been good to use more time, but after lunch Carl always needed the toilet, and so they'd drive from here up North East Valley to Bethune's Gully where there were public toilets and a short walk they could do before Evan dropped Carl back at his shared residence.

'Bethune's Gully for a toilet stop, eh mate?'

Carl looked at him.

'Close up the old lunchbox and put it in your bag, eh?'

Evan got the blue school bag from the ground between them and gave it to Carl. As if suddenly the seat was electrified, Carl stood abruptly and started putting the bag on. The zip was undone and the bottle, some sunscreen, and a tennis ball fell out.

'Whoa there, no rush,' said Evan gently. 'No rush, mate.'

With the bag hanging from one strap, Carl stood, putting his weight on one foot and then the other. Evan got the lunchbox and the other stuff and put it in the bag. Then he zipped up and helped Carl with the straps.

'Okay, then? Okay, mate?' Evan put his hand out for Carl who responded with his only person-to-person gesture—a fingery low-five. 'Back to the car then, eh?'

It always felt better moving. Walking with the sun lighting the leaves, this, the job, felt easy.

They crossed a bridge. There were patches of lichen.

'Lichen all around here, eh, Carl?' went Evan, stopping

and looking back.

Carl came on. He had a sharp face, a side part and an angled nose. Sometimes his olive-coloured eyes crossed a little.

Staying ahead, Evan went off the bridge. Carl looked like a French rugby player from back in the day. Evan liked him. This here—the bush!—this was his office. The track forked and he stopped again, smiling and waving his arm in the way of someone guiding a small plane.

'This way, mate, this way. Let's get to that toilet.'

The gravel road to the Bethune's Gully car park was dim, pot-holed and one-laned, so Evan drove slow. Carl rocked gently against his seatbelt, took off his sunglasses with a rapid move and ducked his head, looking at where the low branches were thick with leaves.

'Toilet, a short walk, and then hometime, matey.'

The road bulbed to a car park. Low wooden railings, the toilets, an empty playground. Evan parked, turned off the engine, and waited. With Carl, what you didn't want to do was rush from one thing to the next—*You're not a courier-driver* is the way Carl's previous support worker had put it—so Evan always held them a few minutes in the car when they arrived at a new place.

'Okay, matey. Take a breath or two here, eh?'

Carl had put his glasses back on and now he lowered his chin, looking over the frames at Evan.

Sometimes Evan got the feeling Carl knew who he was; other times he was sure it wouldn't have mattered if he was an octopus.

The car ticked. Carl's face was frozen. Under his nose on this side looked red and sore.

'What have you been doing to that nose, mate?'

Carl looked at Evan and then out and up to the blue sky.

'This summer, eh?' went Evan, shifting his feet off the car's pedals.

Since mid-November, Dunedin had been Tahiti. Hot days, hot nights. Kingfish had been spotted in the harbour, sunflowers were sprouting up all over the place. Everywhere you went you smelt sunscreen. At home, after dinner, Evan had got into the habit of going out the back naked with Ed and using the garden hose as a shower. Jo would come out to watch and maybe it was that—the sun, the cool rubbery water—or maybe it was them both going to bed naked, or maybe it was that finally Ed—at ten months—was sleeping through the night, or maybe it was all the stone-fruit they were eating, but whatever it was, suddenly, after a long period off—Jo was pregnant and then sore from the birth and then tired from being up overnight—Evan and Jo were screwing endlessly.

Caught up in what they'd done last night, Evan released his seatbelt with a flourish. 'Bethune's Gully, Carl. Back at Bethune's, eh?'

Straight away he regretted his enthusiasm because it had given Carl a surprise and now Carl made a noise, a deeper one than Evan had ever heard before, and rocked hard against the seatbelt, tugging at the door handle and flying open the door.

'Easy,' said Evan. 'Seatbelt first, mate.'

But Carl got worse. Gritting his teeth and slinging forward so that his sunglasses came off.

'Hey, easy. *Easy.*'

But Carl again went hard against the seatbelt which this time locked. His eyes bulged, a choked-off sound coming out his nose.

Evan pressed the release button on the seatbelt and Carl opened the car door and rocked out, onto his feet and away from the vehicle in the direction they'd come.

Evan got out fast too, following Carl, who was hunched, and walking more with his hips and lower back than his legs so that he sort of undulated.

'Carl? Carl? *Mate*?'

Carl stopped. The muscles in his neck were tight, carrying his head forward and low.

Worried about an attack, Evan stopped off to the side a bit. Along with his weird neck position, Carl had both hands at the front of his pants. This was something else the previous support worker had mentioned.

'Okay, mate,' went Evan, getting close and gently turning Carl. 'Okay, the toilets, they're this way.'

They crossed the gravel. Still with his hands down there, Carl made a long low noise, causing a kererū to shift in a cabbage tree by the toilets and then fly up the gully. Far away a dog barked out a response. Otherwise, in the heat, everything stayed dead still.

'This way, yeah, that's it, we getting there mate, good on you, good on you.'

But something was off about the toilets. Both doors were held open with chunks of concrete block. Tape—that red-and-white *DANGER* kind—lay on the ground around one of the doors.

They went to the one without the tape and looked. It was gloomy and smelt bad and it took Evan a moment—the toilet, the place to piss and shit, was gone.

'There's just a hole,' went Evan.

Carl started to go in. 'No mate, let's try the other one,' Evan said, getting Carl by the shoulder, reversing him gently, showing him towards the other door.

A fat fly welcomed them, thumping into the ceiling light that was on, despite, again, no toilet.

Ahead of Evan, Carl went forward, taking down his shorts and turning as if to squat.

'No, mate. You can't. There's nowhere to go.'

But Evan thought of letting it happen. The piss and poo would go close enough to the hole. If they had to they could wash their hands in the stream that ran out of the gully. It must be no more than an hour to go—get this done, go for a walk, and then home time. There was no toilet paper, though! How would he clean Carl's arse? And what if Carl slipped and got lodged in the hole?

'No. No, not in here.'

Carl looked at Evan and started swinging his hips back and forward. His shorts and undies slipped loose, making a pool over his shoes. He looked at Evan and then back and down, as if somewhere to sit might suddenly appear.

Instead of acting, which he knew he should do, Evan got out his phone. Fifty-five minutes.

The fly hit the light again and then flew past into the heat. Stalling, really nervous now, Evan turned and watched the thing's flight path.

Carl made a loud urgent noise in the back of his throat.

Forrester Park, the sports grounds down from the entrance to Bethune's, it would have to have toilets. 'C'mon Carl, let's go. We'll find somewhere else.'

Carl dipped into a deep squat, found nowhere to sit, stood straight, and did the hard, long noise again, fluttering his fingers out from his face as if *they* were the noise. Then it stopped, replaced by a long fart and urine, out onto his shorts and undies.

'Carl,' went Evan, going forward. '*Carl!*'

The piss stopped, sputtered, and then started again. Evan took off his cap, and in taking it off, thought to use it. Squatting, he held it under Carl who made a different noise and then started pissing more freely. In the cap it pooled briefly then started leaking through the vents.

Evan adjusted the cap's position and held Carl's shorts clear. 'Sorry, mate. Sorry about this.'

The flow stopped.

'You done, mate? Is that it?'

Evan looked up at Carl who was watching the light.

There wasn't shit, but there was the smell of it. So, either let him crap down the hole—and possibly down his legs, onto his shoes—or try and get him to Forrester. Whatever Evan did, with Carl's raised state, his movements and noise, the feeling was that violence was close. It made Evan scared. Hair-pulling would eat deep, keeping him awake all night. Already he was composing the email—subject line: Resignation. *Sorry, but I'm not staying in a job that includes being assaulted. I'm not paid like a policeman. I'm not a soldier!*

Trying to squat again, Carl glanced Evan with his knee.

Evan stared at the space between Carl's legs where shit would come, where it would splat, where it would just run and run, but nothing came. Carl was holding on, his face small with the effort of not shitting. Though his brain had put his body in position, it was also saying *don't*, and the effort of that was pressing close the features of his handsome face.

And hold on. This wasn't the old days—with Ed, with Jo still having two months on maternity leave, with their mortgage, Evan couldn't let his job slip down a hole.

'Not this hole, Carl,' went Evan, abandoning the hat, and standing at the same time Carl stood, tugging up his shorts. They were wet in patches, but not soaked. In this heat, with a bit of a walk, they'd dry off. He could get through this. He could.

'We can get through this,' said Evan, looking at Carl who made another urgent sound.

'Forrester Park,' said Evan, and then in a stronger voice—the previous support worker said *sometimes be firm*—'C'mon mate, outside with me. Now.'

Standing, he went out into the day. The hot air was clean and fresh and when he turned, Carl was there, still undulating a bit as he walked, but coming.

'Good on you, Carl, good on you mate.'

Because able or not, who wanted to need the toilet and think you were about to go only to find nothing but a hole? Carl needed him. Right now—obviously!—but also, week to week.

Evan felt better—a bit less scared, a bit more

determined. Though Jo didn't know everything about him, she was aware of his catastrophic thinking and she said he needed to do better at 'reframing'. That sometimes he had to turn his thinking inside out. So, then, well . . . this was a chance at heroism. A chance to really help Carl—not just burn time wandering isolated tracks, driving back and forth across the city, and sitting for ages while Carl ate his lunch.

'Okay, to the car,' went Evan in a clear, firm voice, like it was a cop show they were on. Not that he wasn't totally dry all the way down his throat, not that, with his nerves up everywhere else, he couldn't feel his feet—instead of Asics it felt like kayaks he was standing in.

'Let's find out what they have for us at Forrester, eh mate?' he said, guiding Carl into the car, trying to be quick but also calm, trying to keep the mood light and conversational.

Evan went around the car fast and got in, started the engine, reversed, turning the wheel hard, and then accelerated out of the car park, so that Carl went back and then forward, and then, as if saying goodbye to the gully, he yelped, fluttering one hand in front of his face and grabbing the front of his pants with the other.

'Okay,' said Evan, enjoying the car's motion. '*Okay.*'

The clock on the dash wasn't accurate. He wanted to check his phone, but the one-lane road needed concentration. Bush flashed past. Actually, driving faster on gravel was better—you sort of boated the surface rather than getting dragged down. And it, speed, seemed to be calming Carl, who sat straight back in his seat, his hands on his knees like someone in a First XV photo. Accelerating along a straight length of road, Evan turned on the commercial radio station Carl's support plan mentioned. On came an older song Evan had never liked, but now, after Carl's bellowing, it was a good change.

'Sounds better louder,' Evan said, giving it some volume, before braking hard for the next corner.

'Almost there, mate. Forrester here we come, eh?' he said, rounding the corner and starting up the last little slope where there was a sign and a big wooden archway.

Jo was a nurse. She'd been doing the occasional evening shift, but when Ed turned one she'd be back to full-time nursing. Then—and tonight and tomorrow until 3pm was a bit of a test—Evan was taking over at home with Ed. Financially, Jo had said, in the superior tone she sometimes used, it's the only sane thing to do.

Evan swerved to avoid a low-hanging branch and the car fished across the road, but his hands were light on the wheel, and without losing much speed he had them straightened and flashing towards the entrance.

'A house husband, what do you think mate?'

Carl moved his hands up his legs to the front of his pants.

'Okay, okay, almost there.'

Let there be toilets at Forrester Park. Let it be one great big toilet, with clean sinks, liquid soap lined up in milk-bottle-sized dispensers, paper towels, piped music and an automatic flush. Please, God.

As if communicating to the same being, Carl rocked forward in his seatbelt so hard he stapled over, whiplashed back into his sitting-straight position, and then let go a long, desperate whine.

There was the wooden archway—at the top of the last bit of gravel—and worried about a hair attack, and wanting Carl distracted, Evan floored it, talking over the music. 'A house husband eh, Carl? Can you imagine it? *A house husband*,' he said, making it sound extremely unlikely, like instead of support work, he'd been working on fishing boats, or flying choppers, making it sound as if this move to full-time parenting was going to be a major life change for some heavy-handed, big-whiskered, Kiwi joker.

But before that, here was the archway, and here were the car's back wheels gliding hard into a pothole—into loud, bad, mechanical noise—bobbling them weirdly towards one tall edge of the arch, tipping Carl onto Evan's shoulder, Evan who had his foot on the brake and the steering wheel pulled hard away from where they were going, Evan who made a frightened sound as gravel became asphalt and the tyres gripped, stopping them, kissed up against the arch.

'Carl?'

Carl went off his shoulder, back into his seat, and then forward towards the windscreen, ducking and looking, as if to check the date on the car's WOF.

'Carl?'

The sound Carl made was his gentlest in a while.

Holding his hands off the wheel as if it was the cause of the near-crash, Evan let out his breath and said, 'Did you like that?'

The car had stalled and the music was off. But Evan still talked loudly.

As though they were his ears, Carl covered his knees with his hands.

'Good on you, Carl, good on you, mate,' went Evan, looking back at the heavy, rust-coloured wood where lovers had written their initials. He breathed out and then in, considering whether he'd been hurt. Deep in his body it felt sick and hot and sort of overcooked, while at the surface, just under the skin, cold liquid flowed around his neck and groin.

'Shit,' he said, managing to get the volume right.

It was here that, having nearly had an accident, he'd have usually started talking about what happened. 'Whoa! Shit, mate.' About the car's slide. About how his door was so close to the arch that getting out would mean climbing across the handbrake and gear stick, about how, during the slide, he'd felt his body tense for impact. About how he was still tensed. About how, right now, his brain stem was telling him something was off with the car's balance.

Instead he kept his mouth closed tight over his tongue.

Carl made another soft noise, as if giving in to an idea he'd had, and took off his seatbelt.

Evan pressed back in his seat, shifting one hand to the wheel and the other to the key which he turned. Nothing happened.

'Won't start,' he said, as if Carl might be able to help.

He'd been speeding. The father of a new baby and he'd been speeding along a narrow, gravel road. What if a lorry had been coming the other way? Or a tourist bus? As the breadwinner he'd risked his life so that . . . what? So that the man he was looking after—who he was *supposed* to be looking after—could do a shit. Was he so afraid of having his hair pulled? And now what? The engine was rooted. And he had a flat. Actually, he couldn't even get out of the car.

As if his stupidity was ahead on the road he stared. What if he'd been hurt? Or Carl—what if he'd been hurt and Evan had to go to prison? Where would Jo be then? And Ed?

Evan sat. The failed plan to speed had drawn off a lot of confidence. He could ring someone, but who? Could he pay a taxi to take them back to Carl's place? Should he ring Jo? Maybe she could bring their car and wait with Ed while he returned Carl.

He tried the key again. Nothing. Carl made a harder sound. It's possible he then shifted his hands from his knees to the front of his shorts, but Evan pretended not to see, concentrating instead on a fantail that came fluttering in over the windscreen and then disappeared.

Maybe he would resign. Leave Carl and just walk away. He could text his boss and say there was a family crisis: *My mum has died*. Mum had died and he had to deal with her, what do you call them?, her affairs. In the future it would mean being unable put a notice in the *ODT*. And he couldn't tell Jo he'd lied so blatantly. And what if, one day, Ed somehow found out? What if one day, to get out of something, Ed told an employer/partner that he, Evan, was dead?

Carl farted. A bad smell came into the car.

It was a relief something had happened that Evan could do something about and he put his chin to his chest and held his breath. The gear stick—it was in Drive. It needed to be in Park. He pushed it forward and turned the key. Like it was nothing, the engine started. The radio came on loud, bringing his heart up out of his chest. He turned it off and put the car in gear. Keeping the speed low, holding his teeth tight, trying to keep the wheels straight so as not to damage the car's panels, he edged forward.

The fart cleared and they were away from the arch, but there was a whump-whump that got worse if he went fast. He'd get over the hill, down to the flat, and find a place to park. But what about the toilet? Maybe crawl like this to Forrester? While Carl was on the toilet, Evan would change the tyre. He wouldn't be that late—cars got flats all the time. No one needed know about the near miss.

'Let's just get over the hill,' Evan said, more to himself than Carl.

It was steep and he pumped the brakes as though it was ice they were driving. Down on the flat a woman on the footpath watched a child ride a trike. She was in a white T-shirt, the trike had an oversized, tangerine-coloured flag, and everything was lit brightly by the sun. The happy sight—relaxed people enjoying the warmth—made Evan feel better and he came off the brake a little, hoping to coast the hill and get them to Forrester, but nothing had changed about the car. Increased speed made the whumping get louder, so he went back to the brake.

With the steep hill and braking, Carl tipped forward in his seat, his nose almost to the glass.

'Seat belt, mate, put that seat belt on,' said Evan, but Carl didn't move, just looked across at Evan.

'Hold on, mate. You can hold on.'

The boy on the trike had maybe seen there was something funny about the car and he'd stopped and was standing over his trike, waving. The mum had seen too and now she raised her hand in a way that suggested she was going to signal, that she too was keen to let them know about a problem.

Other people around made Evan more aware of Carl's safety. 'Seat belt, mate,' said Evan in the commanding voice he'd used back at the toilets.

And maybe it brought back what had happened at the arch, or maybe it reminded Carl how bad he was busting, or maybe, in the confined space of the little Honda, it disagreed badly with his brain, because what happened was Carl sat back, reached across, and took Evan hard by the hair on the top of his head.

The pain was very specific—some hair come out.

'Carl?' went Evan, letting his head go in Carl's direction, steering one-handed with his eyes just over the dash. It was dangerous—forget Forrester, they weren't getting there like this. Reaching for the brake with his toes, Evan stopped the car. The engine idled quietly. Otherwise there was just their breathing noise and the noise/sensation of more of Evan's hair coming loose. Lifting his body, he managed to get the handbrake on. Pain went to anger. 'Fuck's sake, Carl, stop.'

Carl didn't stop.

With hair-pullers the thing to do is press hard on the hand doing the pulling. With them unable to pull so well, the idea is to then prise their hand free, starting with their pinkie. Evan remembered all this from the Carl-specific training he'd received, and now he tried it, pressing on Carl's hand, while using his free hand to work on Carl's little finger.

Doing that, he got his body around a bit—his head was basically in Carl's lap—and looked up. Exertion was in Carl's jaw and in the part of his neck that Evan could see, but the rest of him was calm (quiet, too) as if the doing of violence was helping with the toilet-urgency. And Evan also felt some relief—his heart was up and all that, but it wasn't as bad as expected—because the attack, the thing he'd feared most ever since starting with Carl, was happening. And though it hurt, Carl was actually less scary now than he'd been for the last thirty minutes.

Plus, now there was a good explanation for the flat tyre/car damage—Carl attacked and he lost control, going into a gutter. When Carl was finished, he'd ring work and explain, asking if someone could come and get them. Maybe he'd get the rest of the day off.

The car stalled, opening up the sound of what? Footsteps, footsteps, and something else. All of it outside but closing in. People, obviously. Probably the mum and kid.

Putting in a lot of energy, but whispering, Evan went, '*Carl*.'

But Carl's grip stayed strong, and now people were outside. There was a woman's voice. 'Hello?'

In Carl's window, behind and above, the tangerine flag appeared. 'Hello?' parroted the child, and then made the sound of a siren.

'You okay in there?' said the woman's voice.

'Mum?' said the child.

Carl pulled harder. After a little delay, more hair went up out of Evan's scalp.

'Shit,' said Evan, wriggling, trying to restrict Carl's purchase on his head by burrowing into his soft belly.

'Careful,' the mum was saying. 'Don't get on your bike. Just stay there.'

Evan worked harder on Carl's fingers—they had to get out of here. If this hair-pulling attack was less awful than expected, surely Carl's reaction to a child would be much worse. Wasn't that the way the universe worked?

'Mum?' sang the voice again.

Evan cleared his throat and tried to speak clearly. 'We're okay. Carl here has a disability.'

In the window, the sides of the woman's hands appeared, followed by her face in their frame.

'Eh?'

Evan let Carl's hands go. 'We're okay,' he said, and then in a louder voice, 'I'm a support worker.'

'You've got a flat tyre,' said the woman.

The flag was to one side of her head, but now it moved. 'Flat tyre, flat tyre.'

'*Martin*,' said the woman, leaving one of her hands on the glass, but disappearing her head.

Carl shifted a little at his waist and farted again. The stink mushroomed.

The woman came back, looking in but not saying anything.

'How old is your son?' said Evan, wanting to sort of blank what was happening and get the woman thinking about something else. Then maybe she'd leave and, screw it, what Evan was going to do then was drive slowly—fuck the rim—back to Carl's. And then *he* was going home—back to his family. He'd been attacked and had a car accident. Maybe he had whiplash. He wasn't working with Carl any more, not for $18 an hour. It wasn't safe.

'I feel like maybe we need the police,' said the woman.

That excited the child. 'I want to see. Up Mum, pick me up!'

The flag started to move fast, as though the bike had got away. The woman disappeared and now, with the gravity of the steep hill—and a little boy's hand—Carl's door swung open.

Stood there was the boy. Arms flecked with what looked like Vivid. His shiny helmet the same colour as the bike flag.

Carl let go of Evan's hair. In response, Evan smiled. 'Hi there.'

Holding the trike in one hand so that the flag stuck out on the horizontal, the mum came around the door. Still lying on Carl, Evan raised his eyebrows. 'Hi,' he said.

Something must have felt off, because she stepped one long leg to the side, so that the boy, Martin, had to peer around her knee.

Moving his head out of Carl's gut, resting it on his thigh, Evan talked over his nose to them. 'I'm Evan, this is Carl.'

Carl farted.

'Oh,' said the child, squinting and shifting his mouth to one side. 'Fart, fart.'

Carl made a long, low sound come up from his chest. The boy—he was three, maybe four—disappeared behind his mother.

'You're aware you have a flat tyre?' said the woman, looking at Carl as if he was a wild animal.

That annoyed Evan. 'Carl's autistic,' he said evenly.

The boy's face appeared. 'Mum?' he said.

'Shhh,' she went, as if worried the boy would come out with something embarrassing.

'But—'

'Autistic people, Carl here, their brains process stuff differently,' said Evan, as if mother and son were a class he'd been invited to talk to.

For dignity's sake, Evan wanted to sit, but at the same time lying this way was stopping Carl move in Martin's direction. Best thing would be to carefully get out, closing the door on Carl. Adding an assaulted child to the afternoon wasn't an option. And so, swimming back for the tarseal—the back stroke—Evan kept his feet on Carl, who flickered his hands up by his face, and then looked from Evan to the legs passing across his lap. 'Let's take a look at the flat tyre,' said Evan, trying to camouflage his weird movements by talking like he owned a garage the woman had pulled up at.

To see better, the boy came further to one side of his mum's legs while she too gave Evan room, also watching. With just his heels on Carl, Evan found the road. It wasn't graceful, but it was working. Now though, Carl let go a long sound, shifting violently in his seat, and Evan collapsed his bridge, corkscrewed and stood, reaching for the door, but he wasn't fast enough for Carl, who'd pinballed up out of his seat, and now stood there, *in* the day, fluttering his hands by his sides like they were two chickens he'd caught.

A loud noise approached. 'Motorbike,' said the boy, going back behind the mum to look down the road.

As if he might make a break, the mum made her arm a barrier, but he didn't move, just pointed.

The motorbike—its rider fully leathered—came on. It accelerated up the road and then disappeared.

'The toilets up there are munted,' went Evan, as if they were what had made the person ride their bike so fast.

Evan had backed up so he was between Carl and Martin. Carl's apple-breath was in his right ear. He felt afraid, but also clear-headed. Carl wasn't a werewolf. Or a lion escaped from the zoo. Carl was a good guy—as good or bad as any other guy. Nobody was hurt or dead, and now that he was around other people who didn't know Carl, who more than likely knew nothing about autism, Evan was starting to experience that glow you get when, in a small crowd, you find yourself expert on something the group shares an interest in.

'I'm Evan and this is Carl,' said Evan, putting his hand on Carl's shoulder.

'You told us that.'

Evan felt Jo would have described the mum as attractive—if they nursed the same ward, say—but he wasn't sure.

'Is he your boyfriend?' said Martin.

'How old are you?' went Evan.

'Three,' said Martin.

'No,' said the mum, as if it was something they'd been practising, 'you're four.'

Carl rocked gently. In a low-key way Evan had his left arm back around Carl's waist, holding him by the shorts. A breeze went up towards the gully. The sound of the motorbike was gone. Actually, being around other people was okay. Evan was aware of Carl, his negative behaviours and all that, but he was also aware of these other people. The picture painted by the previous support worker of Carl around children had been pretty gory—or maybe that was just Evan's interpretation. Anyway, at the moment at least, Carl seemed more relaxed than he had all day.

And some of the way Evan and Carl were relaxing must have transferred, wiping out the worry the mum had been having about the situation. 'Well then?' she went, making a flat smile that suggested she wanted to restart her afternoon.

Evan felt himself relax even more and at the same time get sort of stronger. He'd been attacked, but handled it, and now they were talking to other people: giving Carl social experience. Not that Evan's scalp wasn't still burning, not that he wasn't still hyper-aware of Carl making mincemeat of Martin.

'I like your trike,' he said, nodding at the boy.

The mum put the trike down, resting her foot on the seat in a way that denied Martin any chance of boarding. 'You'll be okay with that tyre?' she said.

Evan had forgotten about it. 'Yeah,' he said.

'You'll probably want to coast down a bit.'

Martin pointed to where the road flattened. 'That's my

house,' he said.

Carl went tense, raised his knee as though practising for a military parade, then relaxed.

'Oh,' said Evan, still holding Carl, but looking where Martin had pointed. 'That's a big house, isn't it?'

Watching Carl, as if it was him who'd asked the question, the boy nodded earnestly.

Carl moved again—forward this time and with more intent—so that Evan had to move with him.

The woman stepped back, again getting between them and Martin.

'It's okay. He's okay,' went Evan, bringing Carl right back so they were behind the gutter, up against the car.

There were those Eighties TV programmes—talk shows or whatever—where there was a keeper from the zoo with a polar bear or a snake, and everything appeared calm and easy until suddenly the animal lunged, scattering the attractive, hair-sprayed hosts. Things now with Carl were good, but Evan didn't want to push it.

'Okay then,' he said, thinking that getting back in the car was the thing, getting Carl into his seat and ringing work: *There's been a serious incident, would someone please—*

Carl squatted deep, bounced his bum off the car door, and ricocheted onto his hands and knees, towards Martin and the mum, the mum who, in reacting, lost her balance—her foot had still been on the trike—and dominoed back onto Martin. Like a fruit pip, the trike shot out under her and up the footpath, and then, in slow motion really, it stopped and started rolling back, past Carl's face, down the footpath.

The mum looked at the trike and then at Carl as though he should have stopped it. '*Shit.*'

Not liking her tone, Evan went forward to help Carl, but going over the gutter he stumbled, groped with his hands, and ended up *on* Carl, like Carl was a horse he was riding.

The boy had got out from under his mum, and now all of them—except Carl—watched. Gaining speed, passing the car, the trike veered left, rattled off the footpath and swung around so that, briefly, and now facing the right way, it paused.

'Yes!' said Martin, darting behind his mum.

In response to that swift movement Carl lunged forward, carrying Evan at the boy, the boy who now started to run, because the trike was off again, gaining speed.

'No!' said Evan, as Carl got out from under him and into his own chase.

Fast, the trike was heading towards the other side of the road where there was a narrow gravel verge and a steep drop. 'Martin,' went the mum, '*Martin*!'

So, they were all running—Martin then Carl, then the mum, then Evan, snaking more towards the road's middle as the trike again changed direction. The road that hit hard against all their feet, making the sound of applause, but over that sound, there was another.

'Motorbike!' shouted Evan, and then, '*Carl, off the road!*' but Carl was going after the boy and the boy was going after the trike.

Evan hadn't been jogging or anything, he'd been running, but now what he did was press forward, wheeling his arms so that the feeling he had passing the mum, shouting, 'Motorbike! Stop the motorbike!', was that he was airborne, that he was a jet of some kind, because loud as their feet were, the motorbike noise was huge, and now they were veering more towards the opposite side of the road where there was that urban sort of cliff—pale clay, a big drop—and here, as the road steepened further, the bike deviated again, wheeling more towards the middle, but none of them could change their line. With it so steep, what they were doing was running to avoid face-planting into the asphalt, and Carl was almost on the boy, who, here, could be killed by a shove, and Evan said, 'No, Carl—' but whatever else he'd planned to say was swallowed by screeching as a motorbike, black and riderless, slid past sparking, gathering up the trike and squishing the tangerine flag at the same time as the mum was suddenly back in the race, getting level with and uphill of Evan who was now level with Carl who now reached for the boy as Evan and the mum also lunged, lifting Martin by his armpits and stopping so Carl was blocked by the boy, so Carl's momentum swung the boy out over the bank—gravel from their feet rattled onto a shed's iron roof—and Evan had to contract all the muscles down the back of his body to swing Martin back into Carl.

Immediately crying, Martin was lifted into his mum's neck, while in a similarly decisive move—as if he and the mum were part of some synchronised rescue team—Evan took Carl's shoulders and walked him two metres down the road, where, level with the house Martin had pointed at, the trike's and motorbike's wheels spun happily under that high sun, and someone, not Evan, but another adult male said, 'Jesus fucking Christ.'

Evan walked out of the house with Ed in a baby-pack on his back. It was Friday now, 11am, and, with the day already hot, later than he'd planned for their walk. What if the boy got dehydrated or sunburnt? Home in four hours, Jo wouldn't be happy returning to find Ed attached to an emergency-room drip.

In the drive, in their car's window, Evan checked the position of Ed's hat. 'Okay there?' he asked.

At ten months, Ed obviously wasn't talking. He could poke his head towards Evan's reflection in the window, though, and when he did Evan responded with Happy Face—popping his eyes, smiling super-wide—but Ed didn't react, just played his fingers over the back of Evan's neck.

'Okay, *okay*. Good, then.'

Here he was again, talking out into the air, but with Ed the feeling was more of his words going into a person, rather than at their surface. Not that Carl hadn't done well yesterday. In the end, after what happened in the mum's house, it was Evan who'd done the embarrassing thing. But anyway . . . Ed's hat was set right, and part of the delay in leaving the house had had to do with finding sunblock, so in terms of handling the heat on their short walk, Ed would be fine.

'Right, right. Away with us then,' said Evan, reassuring himself by talking to Ed in the confidence-giving, go-get-'em tone Jo always used.

Out the drive, to the right, he started in on the steep hill that led to the steps that connected their road in Kaikorai Valley to Highgate, the main artery through the well-to-do Dunedin hill suburbs of Belleknowes, Roslyn and Maori Hill. As if it was a lever, as if it would help with the climb, Evan reached back and held the cool shape of Ed's foot.

The voice, yesterday at the motorbike crash, it had been the rider. Helmet on, visor up, leaned right back as though instead of bike boots it was flippers he was wearing, flapping hard against the road as he passed, his arms wide to the side like a body-builder's, he'd said, staring right at Evan, 'Idiots fucking around on roads.'

Evan had stayed quiet. Confrontations weren't his thing. Even when something really got to him, he'd swallow it back, staying quiet for as long as it took to digest—an hour, a day—like one of those big snakes with a baby deer. Jo said it wasn't good, that eventually, holding down on everything was going to lead to some sort of explosion.

This your own personal raceway, is it? was what Evan wished he'd come back with. Or was that too light? Had swearing been called for? Last night, alone in bed, he'd thought about it a lot. Not nearly crashing, or chasing Carl down the road, or the underhand thing he'd done later in the toilet, but about what he should have said to the man, *You old cunt*, with his moustache and funny-looking teeth.

'A rabbit's teeth, a hamster's,' Evan now said, stopping at the top of the steps, breathing a bit and looking back for Ed with the corner of his eye. Ed who still had his hat, whose breath puffed quietly.

'Good bird, eh? That is steep, eh? Eh?'

Evan had expected to have grown more assertive when his son arrived, had expected not to get so hung up on the sort of negative interaction he'd had with the biker, had expected to have more of the steel of that chopper pilot, that deep-sea fisherman. By now, really, as a dad—didn't being a dad make him a man?—shouldn't he have had access to a hard, confident response, and if necessary, shouldn't he have been willing to back that response with physical force?

Instead he'd stood—cowered, is that the word?—behind Carl, pretending—for the mum, but mostly himself—that Carl needed his focus, that people like the biker weren't worth the time.

Closing on Highgate, the road lost its steepness, and stopping beside a parked SUV, Evan reconfirmed Ed's hat position, and then walked on. Ahead, a scooter went past and Evan swallowed—*Forget about it*, that's what Jo would say—and said, 'Scooter, mate,' and then, 'Van, a van,' and when that vehicle had passed, it was all quiet, just a supermarket bag tied to a drain's grate, just two kererū resettling themselves on a powerline.

'Highgate, we're making a right onto Highgate,' went Evan, cornering, checking which side of the road—it was wide, empty of people or vehicles, and roasting—had the shade.

The man had freed his machine from the trike, kick-started the engine, looked up at them, shaken his head, and then taken off.

'Arsehole,' the mum had said, still holding Martin who

by then had moved from crying to heavy nose-breathing.

With the man gone Evan had said, 'Fuckin' wanker,' in a voice he'd never have managed if the rider was still there.

Legs tight around her waist, the boy turned in his mum's arms to look.

'Sorry,' said Evan. And it was then, inside that apology, he realised *he* was busting, that he had been for a while, probably since back at Bethune's, maybe since Ross Creek, and that the energy he'd just put into chasing Carl down the road, driving so fast and being so commanding outside the broken toilets had come from the fact that he, unconsciously, knew that without Carl organised, there was no way *he* would ever get to a toilet.

'It's okay,' went the mum, smiling away the word he'd used. 'Thanks for helping with Martin. You're faster than I'd have thought.'

Then she had looked and stayed looking, as if in giving the compliment she was expecting something of her own, but what Evan said—operating deep within the frustration of his own lack of assertiveness, and being coached hard by the urgent shivering messages coming from his bowels—was, 'Carl really needs the toilet, is there any chance—'

He stopped talking and smiled, gesturing at her house. Carl bobbed as if about to squat, but Evan just ignored him. With his own needs suddenly so high, it was hard to take Carl seriously. Plus, as Evan reflected now, at that time in the afternoon, after everything that had happened, he'd been experiencing a sort of godlike power over Carl: he'd wrangled him this far, keeping him safe, stopping him from killing the boy. Carl had felt tamed. With just a touch and a soft word Evan could get him out of his squat and standing quietly, which was what he'd done, just said, 'Not yet, Carl,' and gently squeezed his shoulder so that Carl stood up and waited, alert but calm, like some sort of animal trained to help a deaf person or someone with no hands.

The mum's expression had suggested Evan's request wasn't exactly what she was expecting. 'Oh—'

'We've got a *big* toilet,' the boy had said, then made the siren sound he'd made earlier.

Aware of the hot sun, Evan walked to a tall hedge and its thin line of shade. Far down the road, as if approaching across a desert, a truck appeared. Closer by, a familiar early-model BMW—it belonged to the local postie, Evan sometimes saw it parked near their house—nosed forward at a Give Way. Around the same corner, an older woman appeared.

Walking with Ed, Evan liked passing other people. Ed with his floaty hair, single tooth and over-size cheeks, and youngish, trim-enough-Evan who, whatever the mum had said about his speed, wasn't in bad shape—*real*, that's how Jo described him—anyway, with the baby-pack that was secondhand and, to Evan, rugged-looking, he liked the contrast he imagined them making—the angel and the outdoorsman—and the idea that strangers would probably place him in the vital role of caring for the boy while the mum rested/worked. Plus with the baby clean and sun-safe, and the open way Evan had of talking to the boy, of stroking his feet and hands, they'd also see he was kind and gentle, and that though maybe he wasn't getting around in shirt and tie—signing deals, bringing home big pay cheques—he was that other sort of man who helped with nappies, who cleaned, who'd often be found in the kitchen, blending meals for the baby or filling his wife's sandwiches with lactation-enhancing superfoods.

'Morning,' Evan said to the old woman.

But she didn't answer, just made a big deal of moving across the footpath as if Evan had a fridge he was wheeling out in front.

Evan walked on. 'Friggin' old prune,' he said. Then, aware there'd been an edge in his voice, he tugged Ed's toes and sang the phrase into song.

Ahead, the BMW passed the truck and kept going, past the daycare, towards the church. Evan stopped singing. 'Truck, eh? *Big* truck,' he said, and then held his breath against its dust. Ed shifted on his back, following the sight and noise, and here the footpath started a gentle climb to the brick church. Evan crossed the road, stepped the gutter and went on.

The house—Martin's—was big. Barn-big, with wide-open double doors that looked over a deck where there was a paddling pool and more bikes.

'Down here, down this way. Show them, Martin,' the mum had said, pointing Evan and Carl in the opposite direction to the sunlit, colourful deck, towards a door. Martin reached onto his toes and pulled the handle, and Evan followed, sitting back hard into his bum cheeks—tensing them, and every other muscle in his body, around his anus—while at the same time, in a tightly controlled voice, he went, 'Lovely house,' and 'Thanks Martin,' and

'C'mon, mate, this way,' as he steered Carl out ahead, down a short wide hall, towards where Martin was now sliding another door, and then, there it was, a clean toilet, carpet, shining taps and a weirdly shaped bath tub, and while Martin was saying something about coming to look at his bedroom, Evan got Carl in, and before he'd even really nibbed the door he was pulling down his shorts, squatting and rotating as if about to throw a discus, aiming to sit flush on the toilet and let loose, but *oh fuck*, he had to stand straight away, because Carl was there—shorts around his shoes, he was at it already—and Evan stood fast, trying to bring back the thing that was happening, but it was too late and in getting his shorts up in order to step safely into the bath—to save the carpet and make use of the drain hole—he tripped, fell into Carl and then down onto the carpet, shitting into his shorts.

By the brick church, Evan lifted his foot to a low concrete retaining wall and tightened his laces. Beside him, the glass bus stop was empty but for a sunny sort of poster stuck to one wall, advertising a support group/language class for refugees. Brown-faced people at a table, smiling. A website address wormed among their resting hands like it was something they were eating.

'Refugees, eh, Ed? Maybe I could do that. Maybe I could help?'

Pushing air from his pursed lips, feeling back for Ed's feet, Evan started walking again, soon making the hard right that signalled the beginning of their return home.

From Epsilon Street there were views south to Taieri Mouth, views too to the huge, heavily housed hill that made one side of Kaikorai Valley. He walked past a For Sale sign, studying the photo of the estate agent. In the window of the house a man worked on a computer. There was a van out in front filled with all sort of tools, a wide broom with fierce-looking bristles and a blue-handled machete in some sort of scabbard. The man in the window looked but Evan avoided his eyes, rounding a station wagon that was parked half in, half out of the next house's carport.

Really, wouldn't it be something if what Ed remembered of growing up was his dad making the city more welcoming. Helping/befriending people who'd escaped war, who really understood suffering—not only teaching them English but teaching them how to be Kiwis. It would be voluntary, of course, but that would make his contribution shine even brighter. Maybe one day Ed would see him receive an award. Well-dressed, he'd stand before a packed, high-ceilinged room, delivering a speech, while Ed—combed hair, neat little shorts—sat front row with Jo.

'Mum,' said Evan, thinking about her, 'Mum, eh? She's home soon, yes she is, Ed, yes she is.'

About the next house something was different. Shirts. Hung from clothes hangers in the lower branches of a big tree. Beside the tree stood a stepladder. Evan stopped. 'Shirts, Ed,' he said, expecting the strange sight to complement his positive feelings, but instead he experienced rage. Had they heard of clotheslines? Or clothes horses? What were they saying, decorating the tree like this? Did it have something to do with the unusual summer? Was it a statement? His throat shifted—was he going to scream? Then—it took a terrible effort—he swallowed, relaxed his fists and kept walking.

Probably it was all the sun. He'd only had coffee that morning—probably he was hungry and in need of water. 'Probably it's not getting enough sleep. It's a stress-hangover from Carl, the car accident, the responsibility of looking after you.'

Out the words floated, harmlessly on the air, but listing things seemed to help—the rage went out of him as fast as it had arrived. A cat crossed the footpath then stopped, making a semi-circle around a power pole. Otherwise there wasn't another body in sight. 'Maybe I've been having too much sex,' Evan said. 'Or maybe without it last night, all my hormones got badly blended.'

He reached the top of a shallow hill and crossed. Ahead, forward-facing, was the postie's car. The driver's door was open, winged out across the narrow road, while the postie—wiry with grey hair that made a glittering oval for his tanned bald spot—did something with a large piece of brown paper at the front wheel.

'Our postie,' said Evan.

After it was over, after he'd wiped his own and then Carl's arse, after he'd toppled the shit from his undies and shorts into the toilet and rinsed those clothes as well as he could under the bath tap, and then given his and Carl's hands a good soapy wash—after all that, standing there sweating in the stinking room, Evan had made the decision to swap shorts with Carl.

Eleven-thirty. Jo was home in three and a half hours. A funeral. She'd be sad. Maybe. Or distracted? Maybe she'd be in that happy-to-be-alive state death sometimes got you in and being back with her own little family might make her euphoric. Whatever she was, Evan would put all his focus on her—giving a good rundown of what he and Ed had been doing since their morning texts/phone call. He wouldn't mention Carl. They'd talked last night and this morning and not once had she asked about his day. No doubt, in her mind, all his days were the same. Though really, about yesterday, there wasn't much to tell. Especially if you cut out what reflected badly on Evan. But then, there was a lot he'd done well.

'Evened itself out in the end, eh, Ed?'

Something moved the air behind Evan and he stopped. In blue and white stripes, Ed's hat was on the footpath. Setting for the squat, Evan bent and picked it up. Standing, he felt light-headed, but it passed quickly and he walked on. Ahead the postie's low position in relation to his car and the paper—was it paper?—was unchanged. Evan stopped beside a Jeep, starting the process of getting the hat back on.

In the toilet, trying to sound cheery, Evan had said to Carl, 'Pull up those shorts, that's it, mate.'

They'd got stuck passing over his knees and Carl had almost fallen.

'Whoops, yep, that's it, Carl, get them up. Oh yeah, they look okay. Real good, in fact.'

Evan stood in the mirror with Carl. Brown on different parts of the shorts with a wet-shit smell. Looking, anyone—even Martin—would know what had happened. But what should Evan have done? If Carl hadn't got to the toilet first, wouldn't the picture have been the same?

Evan had got angry then—hot and angry, like just now with the shirt-tree—and been too rough trying to stretch Carl's T-shirt down over the dirty shorts, causing Carl to again lose balance and make a sound that Evan, thinking back, realised was Carl being scared. Not that the tugging achieved anything. It just meant Evan had to re-wash his hands.

Still the postie was on the road, crouched by his front wheel. A flat tyre? Evan had experience with those! He'd say, 'Gidday,' and maybe offer some advice. Hopefully they could chat. Or yarn—yarn's more masculine—about the summer or the man's job. Evan could ask after the decreasing quantity of mail these days—because all the alone-hours, all the talking without response had his brain feeling sort of dry and clumped, like when he buggered the cooking of spaghetti and *it* clumped and Jo really looked at her meal before starting to eat.

'Gidday,' went Evan, too loud and with a little anger.

But his volume didn't matter—just then a car, a station wagon, came up behind the postie's car and tooted, because with the narrow road and the postie's door the way it was there was no room to pass.

The postie stood, looking hard at Evan as though he was the thing tooting. Then, figuring it out, he said, 'Hold your ruddy horses,' and closed the door, then pressed himself against it as the station wagon passed. The thing at the tyre caught Evan's eye. A wing, the inside of a big brown wing, shaped out and up from the wheel.

Another effect of the brutal summer was more hawks. Though it had been hot on the coast, the heat inland—

the Maniototo, Central Otago—was brutal, and so, more and more, you saw them perched on swing sets, kiting up above the suburbs, roosting in the tall pines at the Botanic Gardens. People had written letters to the *ODT* worried about their pets, just as concern had been expressed about the dwindling pigeon population in the Octagon, but most people—and Evan was one of them—reckoned the birds added to the city's personality.

But this one wasn't adding to anything.

'Shit,' said Evan, looking at the postie.

The man didn't say anything. He was tanned and small, older than Evan had realised. His red polo darkened by a deep necklace of sweat, he crouched near the wheel.

Evan went closer, right up to where the postie was trying to put the two parts of a jack together. And there—on its back—was the bird. Mustard-coloured eyes, hooked beak, legs like pale-yellow sticks ending as curved scissory talons. There was no blood. The only noise was the scratching of that free wing against the asphalt.

Ed shifted.

'Bird,' said Evan. 'Hawk.'

The postie looked over his shoulder. It wasn't just that his hands were shaking or even his arms, it was his whole body. And sweat was coming up everywhere. Pilling on his bald spot, dripping from his ears. The bird strained towards him—or towards the pain—spreading its talons and opening its mouth. The postie flinched, still trying to thread the hooked end of the handle through the main body of the jack.

'Could you—'

Evan knew that tone. Sometimes getting a nappy on Ed was hard for Jo. He'd scream and thrash and she just couldn't get them fixed right. Evan always managed it—and the more successful he was the more confident he got, while Jo kept losing confidence. Not that she liked asking for help, always cutting off her request and deploying the same tone the postie had.

Evan liked when it happened, but he always kept his expression neutral when she handed him the nappy. Same with now—just held out his hands, taking both parts of the tool.

The postie stood and, freed from his discomfort, he made a show of giving Evan room, gesturing to a place beside the bird and wheel as if Evan was someone he was introducing to the lectern at a funeral. 'I was texting my brother,' he confessed. 'I didn't see the bird.'

Not used to being talked to, Evan just nodded.

'Kevin, my brother, he's in hospital,' continued the man, as if Ed's silence held some power over him.

'My wife's up at a funeral,' went Evan, like the two situations were shared ground.

The postie nodded. They both stood in the road and looked at the bird.

Broken wings on birds of prey—it wasn't like they could put it in a cast. Still, you never knew, maybe it was just pinned. Maybe when Evan got the wheel up it would take flight.

Evan's daydreaming enraged Jo and it seemed to have a similar impact on the bird, which spasmed again, screaming silently.

The problem was Ed. Working the jack would be hard with him on his back. And the heat—Evan didn't want him out in the sun much longer. But remembering yesterday and the refugees, he wanted Ed to see him *do something*, to see him as more than just the man who went off to work unshaven and in old clothes. Not that Ed would ever remember! But Evan would. Success would strengthen his foundations. After yesterday, after what the mum had said, that—strengthening—was really needed.

Evan braced himself and squatted. Again the bird flinched, but with the way the tyre had him there was no way he could attack. Feathers stuck out near Evan's hand. He put the parts of the jack down and touched them. 'It's okay, mate,' he said, trying a confident tone. 'We'll get you flying again.'

'You think he'll be able?' went the postie, like Evan was some sort of expert.

Easily—why had the postie had so much trouble?—Evan fitted the two parts of the jack together and put it down for a test run. It was small and heavy and when he worked the handle the mechanism moved smoothly.

After the mum's house he'd had to change the tyre on the work car. With Carl sitting on a plastic shopping bag on the passenger seat, he'd coasted to the flat part of the road and got it done. It had taken some time—he'd had trouble with the lugs—but he'd got there and having done it recently, and with the postie so grateful and deferential, Evan's brain began to shift from shirt-tree rage/self-doubt towards a happier feeling of general mastery.

Now he needed to find a good place for the jack. That

would mean getting very low and no way was that working with Ed on his back. Leaving the jack, he stood. Sweat dripped off his face. 'This heat,' he said.

Looking worried, as though he was about to be abandoned, the postie reacted as if given an order. 'An umbrella,' he said, 'for shade. There's one in the boot.'

Evan looked for a good place for Ed. He could stay in the baby pack. It had aluminium struts you spread, making a base for the canvas nest.

'Just have to put him on the footpath,' said Evan, unbuckling the chest and belly straps and taking off the pack. The postie took an umbrella from the boot.

Evan set Ed down near the front of the car. His hat was still in good position and, as always, he grinned at Evan—thrilled after only twenty minutes just to see his dad's face. Evan grinned back, touched his son's reaching fingers and then stood with the postie who now also had a bottle of water. He opened the umbrella and raised his arm. Shade fell.

'A drink?' he said, showing Evan the water.

It was sort of like being a sports star—a boxer or cricketer—and though Evan had both hands free he opened his mouth. Aiming, the postie fired off a jet of water.

It was good and cold. 'Aah,' went Evan, and then, sort of getting into the master/servant thing, he said, 'Keep the shade on my boy. I'll jack up the car and get the bird.'

Against his bare knees the road was soft and warm from the heat. Moving felt so easy without Ed on his back and dragging the jack under the car onto the hawk-free side of the wheel, Evan was filled with a sense of capability. How good was it to have someone around who reacted when he talked? He was soaked in sweat, but also in this feeling of being respected. Could *this* be his job? Going around helping people in need?

Further down the car, nothing could save the hedgehog. Crimson, glistening, sort of piled upon itself. Evan looked nearer by for a flat plate of metal to set the jack beneath. 'You're okay, mate, it's okay,' he said, communicating with both the bird and Ed who'd started some of the sounds that preceded serious crying.

Yesterday, at the mum's house, while Evan had tried to creep Carl to the front door, Martin and the mum had been on the deck. But Carl had made noise and Martin had looked. He'd been eating an extra-long ice block. Evan had raised a hand. 'Well, okay then.'

Wearing what looked like his mum's running shoes, Martin waddled in. 'What's that?'

'What?'

His frozen lolly held like a light sabre towards Carl's shorts, the boy stepped out of the running shoes. '*That.*'

'That's nothing,' said Evan.

The mum came in smiling. She was wearing sunglasses. Trying for a distraction, Evan said, 'Still hot out there?'

A riddle she was pleased to have solved, she said, 'You two have changed shorts on us.'

Raising his eyebrows, as if up until then only he'd been in on the joke, Evan said, 'Okay, *o–kay*,' and tried to get Carl moving towards the front door.

But Martin came on, using his weapon to block their

path. 'Poos? It's poos. POO ALERT!'

Moving in front of Carl, Evan held up his hand like a policeman. 'He shouldn't get too close.'

'Why?' said the mum.

'He bites. Sometimes he attacks children.' Guilty and nervous, Evan's words came out fast and hard.

The mum took off her sunglasses. 'But you brought him in anyway?'

Unsure what to say, Evan went back to raising his eyebrows.

Carl bucked gently and made a noise and the mum swished Martin out of their path, to the far side of her hip.

'Right,' said Evan.

'No, *no,*' said the mum. Then she took a breath and counted three questions with the fingers on her right hand. 'What's your full name? Where do you work? Why is this poor man wearing *your* shitty shorts?'

Her intensity had got Martin crying, which was what Ed now started doing, but it was okay, the jack was ready to go. Evan had it positioned, even raising it a little so it began to take some tension. His plan was to get the postie to raise the car while he held the bird. Needing to comfort Ed and explain that, he came out under the car. Seeing him, Ed cried harder. Still with the umbrella, the postie had a foot on one of the pack's supports, stopping it toppling.

Evan went over to Ed. 'It's okay, mate,' he said. 'It's okay.'

He kissed Ed and tried to cuddle him. Ed's shirt was damp. His face was red. He bobbled, screaming harder.

His hat came off.

The pack had a looped strap system that linked together with a plastic buckle at Ed's chest. 'It's all right, I'm getting you out,' said Evan, fumbling with, tugging at, and—you could probably blame all the adrenalin—snapping off one of the three prongs that made up the insertion part of the attachment. Finally unlooping Ed, he lifted him out. It was like cuddling a roast chicken. Where his hat had been was hot and wet. 'Shoosh, little man,' went Evan, 'shoosh.'

Not knowing what to say or do, Evan had answered all the mum's questions. She'd listened, not writing anything down, just looking pleased with herself as if his giving over the information was punishment enough. Then, maybe remembering the threat Carl posed, she herded them out of the living area. 'What sort of men are they?' the boy, Martin, asked. Not viciously or anything, just curiously, as if his own dad was a whole other species.

Wanting to leave on good terms—and thereby reduce the odds of the mum calling work—Evan looked back to say something, but she was right in close and all he saw was her stony face, so he turned back, reaching around Carl for the handle to the door, and when it opened—the blue sky, the brilliance of a flowering kōwhai—Carl let out a loud happy bellow.

It must have startled the mum, or maybe she'd planned to say something like it anyway, because, parroting her son but using a really hard voice, she said, 'Yeah, what sort of man are you?'

Evan hadn't answered—he didn't know. Maybe Jo could tell him. Actually, what she'd be telling him now was to get Ed home. Because he was really crying.

'Shoosh Ed, shoosh little Eddie-boy.'

Down a bit, around the corner, onto the steep steps, all the way to their front door. They could take a hose-shower together. After cooling off they could run water through the leaves and pods off *their* kōwhai tree, watching out for fantails, slaters and bellbirds.

The jack was set up. He'd done that. Couldn't he just leave? Shouldn't he?

Evan started to move away from the car. But hadn't he been a hero yesterday? Saving the boy? And actually, hadn't his 'Carl fear' proved wrong? His scalp still tingled, but wasn't that pain easier to take than the anxiety beforehand? What actually was fear? Just *not* doing? Freezing in the face of something scary? Maybe, when you acted, fear was blown clear? Wasn't it much better yesterday when he'd accelerated on that gravel road? Wasn't it much better when he'd been sprinting after Carl and Martin?

Jo would also know about fear—as a nurse she knew a lot. It was just that sometimes Evan would've liked her to use a different tone when explaining things. Not that he'd heard her complaining lately—with his tongue up there between her legs.

That thought got him standing straighter and looking back at the bird that was signalling with its free wing. Four hands were needed to rescue the bird, but Ed was no longer safe in the baby pack.

'We'll have to put Ed in your car,' Evan said. 'We'll put him in your car and while you jack up the vehicle I'll contain the bird.'

'I haven't got a baby seat.'

Evan looked at the car. The boot was still open. 'I'll lay him in there, with my T-shirt, so he can smell me. We'll be fast, though. We have to be fast.'

Evan took off his T-shirt. For some reason the postie did the same.

Cuddling Ed, Evan went to the boot. It was a deep black interior. There was some dust and a tube of shuttlecocks, but nothing dangerous. He laid out his T-shirt. When he set Ed down, Ed screamed, as if it was a frying pan he was going into.

'Shit,' said Evan.

Jo would kill him. Jo would rip off his nuts. Jo would know how to do this in a much safer way, but Jo wasn't here. They had to get the bird out. But what if somehow the wind blew the boot shut and they couldn't reopen it?

'Shit, fuck.'

Ed squirmed and rolled to one side.

The postie came and looked, putting his hand on the boot.

'*Don't*,' said Evan, putting his own hand there.

'I was just looking,' said the postie.

Screaming, Ed rolled back.

Evan's heart thundered up into his head, taking over his brain. 'Fast, come on, fast, raise the jack, I've got the bird.'

He went around the back of the postie and got into position. Normally this bit would have been scary—taking hold of a wild animal—but with the noise coming from the boot, taking hold of the bird's free wing and bracing the trapped wing was easy. The bird pecked hard at the base of his forefinger and blood started, but Evan kept a gentle grip, splaying his elbows to avoid the talons.

'Right?' said Evan.

Even though the postie was in position, he said, 'Right, then?'

Talking exactly like Jo, Evan said, 'Yes, *right*, come on!'

The postie worked the jack. Ed screamed. What if he somehow fell out of the boot?

The bird lunged again, taking more skin. A new wound, beside the other one, shone. More blood pooled.

The postie grunted, sweat hosing off him. The wheel started to lift.

'Yes,' went Evan, 'that's it, yes.'

Ed made a dry, crackling sort of gasp Evan had never heard before.

Panicked, he shouted, 'More!' and then, then the bird was free, pecking him again as he stepped to the side, sliding the injured wing free, getting his hand down the edge of that wing and making the bird into a feathery cylinder he was holding.

'Get Ed,' he said.

The postie had stood and was smiling. 'What?'

'Get my son!'

Again the bird pecked Evan's right hand. His arm was blood.

'Hurry!' he shouted, and then after a moment, 'What are you doing?'

But just then the old man appeared, holding Ed from behind, holding him out from his body as if he was a roll of paper towels, and the sudden environment change—

frying pan to fresh air—worked. Ed's face was wet and crimson and his damp, dusty top made him look like he'd been used to clean down an old piano, but now, looking at Evan, he went quiet.

Smiling at his son, Evan bent and, using the road as a sort of table top, gently turned the bird through his hands to get a reverse grip. Then he stood up.

Mouth wobbling, the postie started crying. 'You did it, mate.'

That set Evan off. Everything backed up in him came splashing down. Carl, switching shorts, what the mum said, but also his love for Ed and Jo. Blood and tears dripped, darkening the road. The bird spasmed. Ed hiccupped.

It returned Evan to himself. 'Keep a good grip,' he said.

'Don't you worry,' said the postie, sniffing, gently wiping his sweaty face on Ed's shoulder.

It was okay. Ed was okay. They'd be home soon. And soon Jo would be there too. He hadn't lost his job. He'd rescued the bird. And not that he was any sort of injured-bird expert, but the hawk's trapped wing had folded neatly in. If it was broken, wouldn't the damaged bones be obvious?

Across the road there was a grass bank down to a house. 'I'm going to put him down,' said Evan.

The postie nodded and said seriously, 'We'll see if he can find his wing.' Then he raised Ed as though there was a crowd he wanted him to see over.

Magnificent. That was the word. Evan felt magnificent. Sore and dirty and sweaty. Like he'd been caving, like he'd spent the day warding off dragons. His wounds stung gloriously. He couldn't wait to show Jo. She'd tend to him. She'd bring him close, cradling his damaged arm. But before that—well, he wasn't just going to set the bird down, was he? Didn't he have to give it a chance? Didn't every living thing deserve the chance at freedom?

Across the road, over the gutter, he threw both hands into the air, releasing the bird.

A scene from the Bible. The baby, the blood, two bare-chested men and for a moment, with Evan's momentum, the bird went up, working with its good wing.

'Go!' howled the postie. 'Go on!'

But then it dropped and spiralled, its bad wing hanging. For a moment, it held at head height, staring at the architecture of the big cranial bone shielding the spongy mass of Evan's brain, and maybe it was something it saw there, or maybe it was the energy the postie was putting into his shouting, or maybe it was the dainty miniaturised hiccup Ed did, but finally the critical brain-to-wing connection was made and with a feathery swish, washing cooler air across the three humans, the bird rose, casting a bird-shaped shadow over the road, while Evan, already back to worrying about Ed and heatstroke, wiped his bloodied hand on his shorts and prepared to take his son from the postie, prepared to turn and keep going.

Bullfighter

Still in his green, supermarket shirt/smock thing, twenty-one-year-old Lance is slumped across the couch with his head on the head-rest. Michelle's there too, at the far end with her hand on his shins, thinking about going to bed.

Advertisements come on and Lance looks over, expanding on what he was saying last break. 'If the PM came for tea we'd serve road-kill as pizza. I'd flip the lid on a Pizza Hut box and hit her with gory old possum.'

The last part of the sentence must sound good to him because he sings it a few times, squeezing Michelle's hand, then something even funnier must occur to him, and he starts laugh-coughing until he's in tears, and his legs sort of cycle, and when he's finished there, distracted this time by close-up hamburger shots of sauce dripping down onions and a glistening patty, he says, mock-astonished, 'Or, Jacinda, what about an invisible omelette? Sorry, we're all out of eggs, cheese, bacon, spuds . . .'

Michelle pushes her hand up between the bottom of his jeans and his socks and tips over so her head's on his hip. 'Spuds, is it?' she says. 'That's what you'd like, eh?'

He smiles at her, his narrowed eyes teary, and then turns back for the movie that's restarted. After a moment of watching, he says, pretty much describing what he's just seen, 'I'd eat coleslaw and fried potatoes on the side of a bacon burger.'

'Mmm, yeah,' says Michelle quietly, because she's been thinking about the same sort of food—crunchy golden nuggets of meat with a shiny, salty dipping sauce—but then, noticing a burny smell—maybe it's just his old jeans or his supermarket smock—if they want it clean, Lance reckons they should pay a laundry allowance—she comes off his hip and says, 'Did you turn off that element?'

In answer, he details the strawberry sundae—real strawberries, none of that sauce-from-a-bottle shit—he'd finish his dream meal with.

One time, spotting hash oil, Michelle bumped the side of the cut-down Coke bottle they were using as a funnel, inhaling a lungful of evaporated plastic (and spewing back down the funnel) so, though she likes a joint, no way does she join Lance in his post-work spotting sessions.

Getting up and going through to the kitchen, she interrupts his thoughts on best/worst sundae toppings with, 'As much as I'd like this place to burn down . . .' but though he's left the lights on and the knives are still inserted in the element's rings, the element itself is cold. She removes the knives and puts them with the empty can of fly spray in the cupboard above the stove.

Seven days a week, between 8am and 5pm, Lance works the till and fills shelves at Countdown. Four evenings a week from 6pm until 11pm he cleans and does odd jobs down at Dunedin Casino.

On his free evenings—tonight, Friday and Saturday—he gets stoned and watches TV. A year back Lance had a car accident and some time in hospital. He wasn't insured and had had a few drinks so there's the court fines and a weekly debt to the other car's owner. Also, there's still payments on his own, written-off car, and payments on a laptop Michelle bought a few years ago but had to sell after the accident.

They're behind on rent and neither of them has credit on their phones. Pay day is Tuesday and what's in the fridge is cheese slices and some carrots in a bread bag. It's clean, though, the whole place is. In the weekends—weekdays Michelle works at the stationery/Lotto store in Mornington—Michelle cleans, smokes if they have tobacco and tries to steer clear of the poker machines at the Mornington Tavern.

'We got any flavoured milk?' Lance says. 'Any of those caramel Magnums?'

She knows he knows the answer, so she stays quiet, looking at the carrot peelings in the sink. Lately, where Michelle's got to—with their debts, and their prick landlord talking eviction and/or rent rise—is that much more of this shit and they might as well do something drastic, something much bigger than stealing a few Instant Kiwis from her work, or getting Lance to nick oven fries from the supermarket. Something more like a bank robbery, say.

'What about robbing the casino?' she says, going back into the lounge.

Lance's got his hands between his knees against the cold. He doesn't say anything and she stays there looking at him for a bit.

'The tellers—where all the money is? What about going

in early one morning and, like, waving a knife around?'

Still looking at the TV, Lance says, 'Then hijack a helicopter and rotor up up and away.'

'Rotor?' she says.

Smiling at the TV, he laughs and she goes over, shuffles him to the edge of the couch, and fits herself in behind. Even if he's stoned half the time, and he's got this pale, caved-in chest, and a funny-shaped nose—like he's pressed against your windscreen is the way he describes it—she's always thinking about him, working so hard at his shitty jobs, and the funny shit he says . . . She loves him, him and his beautiful, purple lips, and so, tucked in behind, smelling the supermarket in his hair, she whispers all that now, except for the last bit, what she does about that, as one of the robots on the TV starts sparking and twitching in a scary, epileptic way, is to sort of scoop and roll Lance, like he's a length of guttering or something, and to start them into the deep, deep, kissing he likes when he's stoned.

The Mornington Shopping Centre—there's the Countdown where Lance works and there's the supermarket's parking area, and down one side of that is a row of shops. On the corner, the Baker's Dozen, then Watson's Lotto and Stationery, Hair and There, Wok on Fire, the Two Empties, as Mrs Watson calls them, and then Party Fairies, which hardly opens these days.

First thing Friday, Michelle gets a few people coming in for their Lotto, but generally, until Mrs Watson comes in at 11am, her main company is the flickering tube light at the end of the narrow store she's just finished vacuuming and dusting. She's floated the till, the dry-cleaning signs are out, and she's unpacked and displayed a box of computer paper the courier must have delivered before she got in.

Michelle does nick stuff—she thought about taking some paper, though what would they do with it?—but she likes Mrs Watson and, overall, she does a good job. Helping customers who've asked for unlined paper or particular types of pens, she always makes sure she smiles and dips her body in a submissive sort of way, trying her best not only to solve their stationery problem but also to leave a good impression, thereby ensuring, as Mrs Watson says, customer loyalty, but really none of that has too much to do with fuck-all, because the only reason the shop exists is Lotto, and the fact that people come from the bakery or the pub across the road to fling loose change at Instant Kiwis.

So where Michelle is now, is behind the Lotto counter, staring at the wee kiosk/bench thing customers use to scratch their tickets or mark their numbers, thinking about lunchtime when she can meet Lance on the wooden seat outside Wok on Fire, where no doubt they'll laugh about last night's couch shag, and the thing that happened with the condom, and maybe, while he's in a good mood, she'll tell him about the power bill and how, two Saturdays back, she took the money he gave her to pay the overdue bloody thing and lost it all on the pokies, or maybe, instead, she'll spend the last few dollars in her account on a sausage roll they can split, and what she'd say, stood there waiting, is she's happy about life—because Lance's in it—but also she's sick of bills and hunger and debt and why *don't* they rob something? What about the BP across the road? What about the stupid pub?

The shop's bell rings as a man comes through the door. Looking right at her he smiles in a kind way and straightaway she lights up her helpful-retailer face, smiling mildly and looking past him to the outside, because, of course, the main chit-chat with new people to the shop is always the weather. 'Still that wind?'

He smiles and sort of shakes himself as if trying to recover from the southerly. 'Ooh,' he says, like it's got into his bones.

Jeans, nice sneakers, a tight-fitting black windbreaker, the sort you might see men wear on their racing bikes, or when they run. He's got a big Adam's apple low in his throat and as he comes over he's still smiling at Michelle, but also around at the shop as if it's a house of treasures or something he's stumbled upon.

'I was feeling lucky,' he says, looking at Michelle in an expectant, childlike sort of way.

She stays quiet, just returns his look encouragingly.

'My wife's birthday today,' he says.

'Nice,' says Michelle.

'When's your birthday?' says the man, smiling, settling his big clean hands on the chest-high counter like it's a piano he's about to start playing.

'May the fifth,' she says.

He's handsome in a what . . . Daddy Goat sort of way? Or what are those splayed-antlered deer-type things? Moose, that's it, big moosey nostrils in a long nose and this money smell. Might be it's his haircut which is tight over his head and like the lines have been ruled. Every month or so Lance goes at his with clippers he keeps plugged in in the bathroom, just so they're ready for him to swipe at whatever doesn't look right at that particular moment. Or might be it's the clear white eyes, when Lance's eyes . . . Well, he'd say himself that, at their best, with all the weed, they're piss-holes in the snow.

The moose, who's been scanning the display of Instant Kiwis and the signs on the counter detailing the different combos you can choose to take with your Lotto ticket, and who now actually makes horns for his head with his hands, says, 'May. A Taurus then, eh?'

How would life be with this guy? thinks Michelle. *You know, just the money part of him?*

'Taurus, that's it,' she goes, not liking the eagerness in her voice.

'Then they'd better be my first numbers,' says the man. 'Those, my wife's age, and today's date.'

It's nothing against Lance, it couldn't be. Gentle, funny Lance. Christ, look how hard he works, and yes, he is smart. He reckons the weed's gobbling up his brain, but there's plenty left to eat. Before the thing happened with his brother, Lance was enrolled at uni—he was going to make something of himself, that's what people who knew him used to say.

And Michelle? Last year of school, a teacher told her she was stronger than she looked. Stronger physically, but also mentally, was the way Michelle took it. Her two front teeth are way smaller than the ones around them, so she'll smile properly for Lance, but that's it. Really, they're the only things she's clear on—her strength, her smile. Them and her love for Lance.

Not that that's stopping her face muscles working her mouth towards a closed-mouth smile. Not that she isn't opening her body a little.

I do not think about other men. She does sometimes, like now, think about other lives. Having a car, say, or one of those credit cards with the gold and the hologram, and the way, in some places, you just wave them near the robot thing that takes the money right out of your account, leaving you to walk out with shoes or whatever.

'And what about—' starts the man; but suddenly the way he's now got his head—tilted idiotically, like she's what, eight?—gets Michelle's brain slipping back to Lance, Lance and his white pipe of a body, Lance and his lips, Lance holding her hand, as always, when they eat, Lance and the problem with her gambling and their power bill, because this isn't a movie, this is Friday morning in bloody Mornington, and so Michelle, ashamed, interrupts whatever it is he's now saying—something about star signs—with a slightly bored, 'You'll want a blank ticket then? To fill your own numbers?'

And here she's called back hard into the shop, because the man doesn't answer, just stands, staring, his mouth a blade of black, as if she's called him dickhead or something, and now she shifts on her feet and runs her finger over the $2 Kiwis because he's still staring, but then he grins, even wider than when he came in, and dips to hold her gaze, saying, 'What was your name again?' like, though offence has occurred, he's prepared to offer her the chance to make things right.

'Michelle,' she says, in the shy voice she remembers using a lot when she was younger. It pisses her off and being pissed off makes her stand differently, but he doesn't seem to notice, just waits a moment longer, his big head hanging there like a horse's, like it's more information he's waiting for. Then, playing his yucky fingers up and down the keys, he says, 'Well, Michelle, you're absolutely right. I plan to fill my own numbers.'

Holding up a blank ticket, she manages a smile. Thinking of schoolteachers, this one's the arsehole who seems awesome to start, but in the end turns out to get their thrills from making you feel like a total retard. 'There's a pen behind you,' Michelle says, in a harder voice, and *finally* he turns and goes to the kiosk where he takes up the pen, fixed by coiled, plastic coated wire to the top of the little plastic counter.

Without meaning to, Michelle makes a fucked-off sound in her throat and the man turns. 'Michelle,' he says, 'come and show me what to do here.'

Doing is always best, as Ms Watson says. And so, back in shop-mode, Michelle rounds the counter, where he makes room in front of him at the bench. It's not unusual. Customers, men especially, seem to have difficulty with obvious shit, like how you need three of the same dollar amount to claim an Instant Kiwi prize, or with Lance, how to poach an egg without blasting the white stuff free from the yolk.

'Mark your number on the horizontal,' she says, showing

him with the pen. 'That's the way the computer reads.'

'The computer, eh?'

And here there's pressure on the left cheek of her arse, like a gate's shut on her. Wiggling free, she turns in its direction, and as fast as she does, the pressure lifts, and now the man's way back, smiling with his hands up, as though there's no way it could have been him.

Wind comes, sheeting rain against the window, moving the door a little, half jingling the bell, and something within the weather gets the man—he's still smiling—stepping forward and taking the incomplete ticket off the kiosk.

'Thanks, Michelle,' he says, before smoothly turning and crossing the shop, opening the door to ring the bell fully, leaving behind the smell of car park and rain as more swishes in from outside.

When the urge to remember has happened, Michelle's looked from the telly to her hands, focusing instead on the lists of hand-related jobs Lance's told her she could excel at: croupier, weather lady, conductor . . .

He's home at 4:15pm and when he's here to help, she'll let it out. It's now 4:10 and she's on the couch with cask wine and cigarettes. The heater is on full, all lights are lit and she's still in her work clothes. Her focus, when she got home, was on squashing what happened with wine, TV and Lance's weed.

Before Mrs Watson arrived, after the creep left, Michelle took two twenties and a ten from the till. Once Mrs Watson had been there a few minutes, Michelle went to the toilet at the end of the shop and pretended to vomit. Mrs Watson asked about it and Michelle started crying, asking if she could go home, though instead she went to the liquor store for the wine and smokes.

Now she hears Lance open the front door. And the opening of the door gets her back to that rain swishing in from the car park. She knew him coming home would start her off, but she didn't know what her emotions would then—

'WHERE HAVE YOU BEEN?'

Like shouting's normal, Lance responds with, 'Mrs Watson said you were sick.'

'HEY!' goes Michelle.

Lance will know something's wrong, but Lance's almost always calm, and in he comes, looking around at the room.

What he'll be thinking is it's more of the usual bad news—bills and shit—and more than her anger or what's happened at her work, what he'll be interested in are the cigarettes and wine.

'Oh, fuck you,' says Michelle, but even in the saying of it, she's off the couch, going towards him.

Lance's always up for a hug and he opens his arms, so she sort of falls into him, but then, straightaway, she ricochets angrily off, away, and into the kitchen.

He comes to the doorway and waits. It's a bright bare bulb they've got in the kitchen, and with the weed in her, what he looks like, stood there with one of her unlit smokes, is one of those life-sized cut-outs of movie stars you see at Hoyts or wherever. That thought—Lance as movie star—makes her smile, which starts her crying.

'Did you nick some money?'

Turning on the element, Michelle jams the knives between the rings.

'Eh?' says Lance.

'SOME *CUNT* GRABBED ME!' shouts Michelle, with such force that something startles and scuttles from one spot of their ceiling to another. They both look, then they look at each other, then Lance raises his eyebrows in the sad way he does, and, finally seeming to understand, he says, '*Eh*?'

Michelle wakes hungry. No lunch yesterday, no tea. The pillow her face is on stinks. The mattress feels sunk and damp like the cupped palm of somebody's sweaty hand. She rolls onto her side and air shifts up from under the duvet. She stinks too. Blinking slowly, she looks past the pillow. From the bottom up, their curtains are rotting. When you vacuum, parts of them actually disappear into the machine. It—the flat—is always worse when Lance's not here. Saturday, 9:20am. He'll already be at work.

Getting up, she goes through the lounge to the toilet where she strips off her knickers and sits to piss. She's still in yesterday's clothes. The smell off them of weed and tobacco makes her want more, but last night, during the talking through of things, they smoked the flat dry.

Finishing, she wipes with a square of toilet paper and then stands. Her mouth feels bad so she goes to the sink and scoops in water. It's cold and good against her hunger and the cleaning feeling of it helps her decide to shower. Reaching past the curtain she spins the taps and then looks at her arse in the mirror. A bruise like a crossed-out word spreads from the point of his attack. The fucker, gripping her like she was fruit. It was one of the things she'd said to Lance before they got to the planning part of their conversation. The first part was more about Lance getting upset/angry. Smoking, he'd walked fast around the lounge, threatening to break things he picked up. Then, when the smokes were gone, he'd started crying.

'But what can we do, Michelle?'

And what *could* they do? Tell someone? With their age and the ratty way they looked, fuck getting the cops involved. And anyway, they didn't know the man's name, they didn't know a thing about him.

'What the fuck are they going to do?' Lance had said. 'Put an APB out on this sporty cunt with an oversized Adam's apple?'

After he'd calmed down a little he became tender—cradling her on the couch—and from there he moved to full-time worry about money, and debts, and if she lost her job they'd definitely be evicted, and then what? Live under a tarp in the town belt?

'I mean, this is all shit and that,' he'd said, but then, shrugging, he'd gestured at their big old spaceship heater as if to say, at least we have warmth, at least we have shelter.

Now in the shower, Michelle soaps under her arms and across her belly, and then just stands, looking at the water coming from the showerhead.

What they'd agreed was that she'd meet Lance at 9:55am at the BP just down from the pub. Somehow, he'd get money from work—an advance on his pay, maybe—

which she'd take to Mrs Watson, who opened at 10 on Saturdays—and confess to the stealing, telling her what happened was down to stress. If Mrs Watson didn't react well, Michelle would tell her she'd had a miscarriage. That she was broke and needed the money to see a doctor.

Turning off the water, Michelle steps onto the mat, dries with Lance's FIJI! beach towel and, looking again at her bruise, swivels her body from one side to the other so her hair becomes a sprinkler, dotting drops on the mirror.

Then the house goes quiet. Or quieter. Like the air was noise and the air's been removed. Pulling her wet hair back, she makes a tight ponytail, and then tries the bathroom light. Nothing. The power. *Fuck*. She goes out the bathroom, down the hall, and into their bedroom. The alarm clock is black. The light doesn't work. In the kitchen, she checks the jug. Nope. Same with the oven. None of the lights work.

Her ponytail drips down her back. The last letter warned of it—their power's been cut.

She opens the fridge. Dark there too. And empty, but for the carrot bag and a folded piece of paper. Lance likes to draw on the toilet. There's paper in there and a pencil, and it's a huge plate he's drawn, laden with hash browns, toast, some love-heart-shaped mushrooms, two eggs, bacon, sausages. Beside breakfast is a glass of juice. Sat on the rim is a bird. In a speech bubble from the bird's tweeting beak, Lance's written *9.55 don't forget!*

'Hi,' says Lance.

Between them a car comes out of the BP. Michelle

waits and then walks, her ponytail cold down her neck. 'Thanks for the drawing,' she says. Then, having thought about food, 'Have you eaten?'

Lance shakes his head. He's pale—the late nights, the weed—and now he coughs and spits onto a strip of grass where a sandwich board advertises three-dollar pies with every tank of gas.

'Can smell the bakery,' he says, handing her two twenties and a ten.

Pocketing the money, she looks at him look up and down Mailer Street like a baddie in a cartoon.

'From the staffroom,' he goes.

'Eh?'

'A handbag in the staffroom,' he says, spitting again.

'A handbag?'

'Where else was I getting it?' He's scared, but it comes out as anger.

'An advance? You said you'd ask for an advance!'

'I asked. Jenna said payroll's in Auckland and even if she wanted to there's no way.'

'What about the tills?'

'What do you think, they leave them open?'

'Tell me you didn't ask for fifty?'

Lance's got his hands way down in his pockets. He starts crying.

'*Fuck.*'

Seagulls come off the BP sign and fly up Mailer Street.

Michelle digs at the notes with the tips of her fingers. Lance pulls snot from his nose, throwing it after the spit.

Breathing out, Michelle catches his elbow. It's bare and

cold. He looks at her and then away. 'Lot of sausage rolls,' she says.

He makes a sarcastic noise.

'I didn't make you steal it. You weren't complaining last night with the wine and smokes. With the weed.'

'I bought the weed. *I* buy my weed.'

When they argue one of the first things Michelle starts on is the amount Lance smokes. Usually he'll come back at her about the hours he works compared to her, but here, instead, he just looks across the car park to Countdown—squatting there greenly under a grey sky—as if he's worried the building itself will leap up and swallow him.

'If I lose this job—'

Feeling past the money, Michelle takes a thin smoke from her pocket—before leaving the flat she'd recycled some of last night's butts with a Zig-Zag. 'Here,' she says, trying to get them back to being close.

He takes the smoke and lights it with the lighter he always keeps in his pocket. Inhaling hard, he wipes his nose and smiles. 'Better get back,' he says.

He turns, checks the road, and then runs, those thin elbows like blades. Michelle watches and then ducks her head into the wind, starting up the pub-side of the road. Another seagull comes in low and holds there, like it's got a question. Across the road, Lance's walking between parked cars in the car park, smoke puffing up out of his face. At Mrs Watson's the sandwich boards are all out and through the window Michelle can see Mr Watson. Saturday's the big Lotto day and though Michelle's asked about it, she doesn't think Mrs Watson trusts her to work when all their profits cross the till. Michelle watches the traffic for a chance to cross. The wind gusts, taking her balance. She sniffs and then swallows. At the supermarket's front doors Lance doesn't stop or look back, just flicks his hand, getting rid of the smoke, and goes inside.

There's a sound behind Michelle in the pub car park and she looks. A man with rolled sleeves loads a vacuum cleaner into a van. The pub will be opening. They'll have the place warm, all the clean beer glasses will be lined up.

When Lance gets home, he'll find there's no TV, not even hot water to wash his face—what good's a clean house without light or food?

The road's finally clear but Michelle stays, turning back to where, finished loading his cleaning stuff, the man gets into his car. Closing the door, he starts the engine and then accelerates out the car park and up the road as if there's something he's scared of. The wheelchair ramp up to the door to the pokie cave. All the water goes out Michelle's mouth and throat, drawing her stomach tight. Wouldn't making more of this money be best? Tripling it, at least. For rent, for Lance's work and Mrs Watson, for power, food, cigarettes.

She could zip in, gamble up a good pot and sort everything out—by tonight they'll be in front of telly eating hamburgers and drinking cold beer. Michelle breathes hard out her nose, going back on her heels. A rubbish truck bangs past, more gulls tip their wings into the wind. Like a compass needle, it doesn't matter how she moves; most of her ends up pointed at the pub. Really, since the power went down, or since she looked at the bruise, probably since she thought about their shitty curtains going up the vacuum cleaner, this is the direction she's been headed.

On the tall stool she sits. The pokie cave is empty but for the recently vacuumed smell off the carpet. Machines around her flicker and chatter. She takes out two twenties. Her machine is Matador. There are the usual jacks, kings and aces, but also higher-paying señoritas with roses in their hair, a glinting gold bar that substitutes for everything but the bulls, white horses in close-up being reined hard to the left, plus those bulls—three or more scattered gets you 25 bonus games—but the ultimate is the handsome, moustachioed man in the brimmed hat. The bullfighter—he's really who you want to see lined up.

Her mouth is still dry. She's always nervous before she starts, but it's worse today. Their lives—not just the power bill—are riding on it. But the lights and noise and colours are such good distractions. Maybe this is what it would be like to do a bungy jump or go scuba diving. All your senses are getting it, so any other stuff falls right back. And now without anything conscious happening—she's done this a lot over the years—her hand goes out from her body and the first note finds the thing's slot as the machine takes over, drawing first that note and then the second from her hand.

With credits up to 2000 she sits back a little, still feeling nervous and sick, but also excited—from here there's the possibility of better life. A beer would be great. A cigarette. If she can get well ahead she'll use the spare ten in her pocket for a drink, but right now, business-like, she starts her gambling—betting 3 lines and 2 credits, so every spin eats her pot down by 6. Jingling, flickering lights, flashing—the bulls don't just come up onscreen, they stampede, hooves thundering, from what sounds like far away to right up close where they snort and paw. Sex would be the other thing—the way you disappear, that full brain impact.

Time is gone. There's the idea of Lance, the man, and their problems, but reality is here. Every few seconds the reels wheel, stopping as they do, slowly enough from left to right—the lag between the fourth and fifth reels is especially long—for her to see the possibility of beautiful big wins building like storms, and, just as fast, to see those same storms fizzle and die.

Michelle plays tactical. Whenever her credits tip her over the original pot of 2000 she'll bet maximum. 5 credits x 25 lines, or around $7 a pop. It's the only way to win big, and she knows winning really big is the only way she'll leave with money. Because once she's in front of her machine, no matter how many credits she gets, it's hard to leave—more than winning, what the machine makes you want is to say close, to keep playing.

'Okay,' she whispers, as one, two, three, four, five jacks line up.

Already she's down to 1500 credits, but this gets 100 back.

She looks at the flashing jacks then presses GAMBLE, setting a single playing card whirling against a glittering black background, blinking first hearts and then clubs. She shifts her forefinger to hover over RED, but then shifts back and taps BLACK. It wins. Now she's got 200 credits. Adrenalin surges, causing her breathing to change and her feet to move a little on the stool's low rail. GAMBLE. This time, quick as, she hits BLACK.

WINNER! 400 credits won, her forefinger shifts to TAKE WIN, but then, in a blur, flicks GAMBLE and then RED, and WINNER! 800 credits! And TAKE WIN gets her to 2300.

'Okay,' she says a little louder, feeling way better than she has for weeks, and for a second she thinks about getting a beer, but instead she flicks 5 credits and bets 25 lines, but that bet loses, and so do the next two, getting her back to 2050. She tries one more big bet, but wins only three 9s on the middle line. Gambling them she chooses RED, when what comes up is black, and already she's back under 2000, and back to 6 credits per spin.

Now a man's on the jungle-themed machine beside her. An older guy with a Coke she can smell. It reminds her she's hungry. Also, she's vaguely aware of her bladder and that her feet feel heavy with blood, lodged as they are on the stool's low bar. Since the man sat, coughing, and then apologising for coughing, she's lost steadily. She was as high as 3560—winning two bonus features in a row—and she stayed above 3000 for ages, betting big and winning some good gambles, without getting any real meaty wins. But now, with him here, she's down to 603 and back to betting 6 a hand. Probably it's past 11am, but maybe it isn't. The machines don't have clocks and there are no windows.

Two bulls stampede in on reels one and two, but then nothing on the third, the fourth . . . or the fifth. Just a queen above a nine above a señorita. Lance knows she gambles, but he's never known the extent. He thinks it's just a few coins—who's he to stop her having some fun now and then? And, anyway, one time she won $80 and got them a huge feed from Wok on Fire. He was home when she got there, stoned and starving, and when she walked in with the two bags full of plastic containers full of noodles and wontons, fried rice and doughnuts he actually wept, getting to his knees and waving his arms and body up and down, calling her 'Golden Arm', telling her to gamble whenever she wanted.

The old man coughs again and then says, 'Righto, beer o'clock.'

He's got a soft, sad voice, and Michelle can feel him looking, but all she does is nod and say, 'Mmm.' Her tongue lies heavy in her dry mouth, and after a moment more, the man must press CASH OUT, because a few $2 coins rattle into the metal tray, where he feels about for them and then leaves.

On the next spin Michelle thinks about betting 125, but sticks instead to 6, and that's good, because the hand doesn't win. Being right lifts her and, when she wins 15 with three jacks on the next spin, she hits GAMBLE and RED and then TAKE WIN, adding 30—or five spins—to her total.

Anyway, what's with Lance's drink-driving? And now he's stealing from handbags? *She* got groped. So what Michelle feels is that she'd win any sort of argument about gambling. And even if she wouldn't, basically what it gets to is we all fuck things up somehow, and this is her way to fuck things up. He works hard, yes, but it's mostly him that's got them here.

One, two, three, four . . . 'Shit,' says Michelle, as instead of a fifth horse, a bull lands on the fifth reel's top line. Still, credits won whirs up to 400 and the only choice is TAKE WIN. With only 408—now 808—credits left, she can't risk a gamble because really, all she wants, more than saving them with a windfall, is to stay here—far from all that other shit—and play.

Now it probably would be past lunchtime. Different types have been in playing. Noisy types, more interested in drinking, who smell of cigarettes, who play a few dollars for fun, and then leave for another drink and their pub burger.

Michelle will leave soon too. 84 credits, 78, 72. Twelve more spins and that's it. Four bulls came up and on the bonus feature she got a line of four senoritas, winning over 2000. But, betting big, she lost that fast. Then it was back up over 3000 with five aces she gambled and won on. Since then it's been water down the drain and now it's back to 6 credits a bet and she can feel her brain having to change, can feel the walls and roof lifting, showing off the real world.

She wins with three tens, but loses the GAMBLE.

54.

She gets off the stool and stands. Her legs are sausages and she smells of the room which smells of chips and beer and the BO off sad, desperate losers like the coughing old man, like her. She's done some long sessions this last year, but this might be the longest. Her machine is warm—her hand's been on it for hours, tipped towards it like it's a synthesiser she's playing.

40 credits, 34, 28.

She wins 24 with queens.

It—her life—comes right back in. There's Lance, and Lance's good, but what if something goes off with him—and something *is* going off, *he's going to lose his job!*—and she ends up alone? Before Mr Grope turned up things weren't exactly perfect, but now . . .

Matador, Matador, Matador, Matador. The fifth reel, the fifth reel, the fifth reel. Matador!

Lights wobble up the machine's ribs. On its head an orange siren rotates. Animated gold coins, treasure of all types, fountain out of the thing's screen. She sits. Back down on the stool.

'Oh, you hit it,' a man says, coming up close, looking, and then, like there's a bungy cord around his waist, returning to his own machine—it's got a bank robbery theme—where, all afternoon, she's heard him whisper-swearing at the losing hands he's been dealt.

TAKE WIN TAKE WIN. She hammers away at the yellow button and her credits run up and up.

10,000.

$200.

Added to what she had it's 10,052.

The machine's jingling has stopped, but it still pulses brightly, waiting for her next move. Behind her, the man swears. 'Where are you, you fucking bank-robbing cunt?'

You can't blame him though, these things are so teasy, letting you get so close! Beyond swearing-man, Michelle hears a truck change gear on Mailer Street. Lance loves her. Skinny old Lance with the funny way he ties his shoes. Whatever way they fuck things up, they'll have each other. She'll bet down to 10,000 exactly and then CASH OUT. Money for Mrs Watson, money for Lance, money for getting the power back on, smokes, beer and food.

She presses 4 credits and 5 lines. That loses and she presses 2 credits on 1 line. Nothing, so it's 10,000 exactly. On the top line two bulls paw and snort. Her finger is hovering over CASH OUT, because she's out of here, taking her winnings to the bar, cashing up, and leaving with $200. She's at the supermarket, putting beer, a family-size pie, oven fries, and a bag of coleslaw on the checkout. But has she really had a good go betting big? Because although $200 is good, $500 would be much better. What about going no lower than 9500?

She stands again, stretches through her back and then turns at the waist. The bank-robbery man, her friend, sips from a glass of beer. He's taking his time. He's not going anywhere. She turns, sits and bets 125, and wham! The Golden Arm. Straightaway five kings! Blinking in blood-red from bottom left to the top of the third reel and then back on the diagonal to the bottom of the fifth reel. 1000 credits won!

Wow! In life isn't there always the possibility of something good happening? Suicide? No way Jose!

GAMBLE this motherfucker. The card flashes red and black. BLACK. WINNER! TAKE WIN.

12000 just like that.

'That's the way to do it,' she says, like she's sat there watching someone else play, like it's someone else playing on.

9000 now, 8875. But she does have a beer—a tall, delicious pint of DB. She'd RESERVED the machine and gone to the bar with the $10 from her pocket. People were talking and drinking. A TV had car racing. It was bright and noisy and the bartender said something she didn't understand. Her hearing was working, it was just that after so much time before the machine she listened for other things. But there, briefly in the real world, she did think of leaving. Going back for the money—she had close to $180—and getting out. By then, though, she held the cold beer in her hand and there was no way she wanted to drink alone, and so she returned and, with half that beer on board, though it's still only her finger moving, she feels she's dancing.

WINNER! A RED gamble on four horses gets 2000.

10,300.

4500.

1200.

The beer's long gone. She needs to pee. She had $200 there for a bit, but now it's no more than ten. What would the time be? 4pm yet? After work will Lance come looking? Probably he'll go to the flat, find out about the power, and then try and find her.

1188. This last bit has gone on for ages—up to 5000, down to 2000, up to 4000. Michelle loses again and then wins 30 with nines. GAMBLE loses and she tries to sigh like none of it matters. Like money is nothing. Like, she's wife to yesterday's bum-grabber, like she's got tons in her account, like if she wanted she could buy the machine from the pub and have it carted off by the cleaner man and set in the high-ceilinged entrance part of her house. Arse-man said it was her birthday—probably he got her jewellery, probably he got a bright red scooter, and right now she was trying to figure out how to keep her hair looking good while still wearing the helmet he got her.

The fucker! The fucker, grabbing her like that.

Two bulls come up on the first reels and she asks God for a third to set the bonus feature rolling, but reels three, four and five stay empty. She flicks her foot forward, moving it for the first time in hours, kicking her toe into the stand part of the machine. But it's nothing to the machine, which just keeps blinking away brightly until she bets again and loses. Bets again, loses. The machine is her bank. It's just that stupidly—*so stupid*—she never takes any money out.

80.

156.

125.

One last big bet, then. Why not?

She stands from the stool. The backs of her legs are

stiff while her knees are soft and, as she bets, she slumps a little, holding herself against the machine, where it's first reel, second, third, fourth . . . nothing.

0.

She stands straight—her legs have come right—and pats her pockets that are empty except for the flat key. She doesn't go, though. On the fifth reel a flashing señorita's got a rose between perfect teeth. Lipstick. A long neck, a low-cut frilly white dress. With the change of position some air moves up through Michelle and she burps quietly.

Suicide. That would be the most realistic theme for a machine. Your bonus feature triggered by three or more gamblers hanging from hooks on doors, the top-dollar prize paid by the blinking image of an old car in an empty car park with a gardening hose wrapped from exhaust to driver's window. Thinking it through, Michelle sways there a bit, like it's her dangling from the ceiling. Then she's out, walking—really, it's more like the floor is moving—into the pub part of the pub, and the light is different, less bright but everywhere. Same with the way the noise hits: laughter, someone going briskly towards a table of men in hi-vis vests with two huge baskets of fluorescent yellow chips, a ringtone that makes her think back to Matador. Why didn't she gamble more? Two gambles on those five bullfighters would get $800! Two tiny touches of GAMBLE and her and Lance are out of trouble.

Outside into cold air and towards her, up the pub's stairs two men jog-walk. They're in shorts and work boots and one keeps whatever laugh they're having going while he looks right at her and then they're gone and Michelle is down the stairs and across the car park which shines under the sun after the rain. Blue sky with no clouds and the wind has dropped. Still walking, moving through stiff hips, Michelle puts her hand against the sun and glances at Mrs Watson's—people are up there, by the bakery, by the Kiwibank cash machine—while her stomach turns towards the smell coming out of the Indian restaurant down from the BP.

Robbing the petrol station, you'd go in with knives and something over your head. But then what? Run? Get on a bus? In movies robbers steal a car first, but where do you start with something like that? Everyone locks their cars, so there's that—just getting in—and then there's starting the engine without a key. Beside a petrol pump a helmeted man's straddling a motorbike. Something about the way he shifts on the seat makes her think of the man in the shop. But she's too hungry to raise the anger to burn up the dead fish he's left in her gut and so it lies there—cold now, awful—as across the road the red neon of Den's Takeaways flickers, and there, walking up past Den's window, it's Lance.

'Lance,' she shouts happily, forgetting for a moment where they're at with her losing the money Lance stole to save her job.

But he doesn't hear—the man on the motorbike is revving it up—and so, watching the road, she runs across Mailer Street, onto the footpath outside Den's. 'Lance?'

He comes up, stops, half waves like she's no more than an old schoolmate or something, and says, pissed off, 'We haven't got power.'

Often when they haven't seen each other properly for a while—especially the days Lance works both jobs—he'll start out being mean, picking at her about something around the flat or saying something hard in response to some bland question she's asked. They've never talked about it, but Michelle figures it's to do with all the hours he works—being stuck too tight in his own head, hating himself for the situation they're in. Usually it only takes a bit of time—a smoke helps—and they're back in the right groove. But whatever its cause, with that fish in her gut and his cold eyes, Michelle's shame comes up her throat, and so, in front of the shop—the place is open, but empty—she unloads. 'Why not give me a hug? Why not keep your mouth shut for five seconds and hug me?'

But she's pissing onto a hot element.

'Did you pay Mrs Watson? What happened there, eh?' goes Lance. And then, tipping his crooked nose towards her, 'You smell of pub.'

'You're a sniffer-dog now?'

He crosses his thin arms like they're all muscled and tattooed.

'What happened at Countdown?' Michelle asks. 'With the money you nicked?'

'I gave it to you.'

'Did you get fired?'

'Did you?'

A man goes around them like they're a traffic island and into the shop. A bell rings there too.

'Bloody bells,' says Michelle, looking at the shop door

and then down at Lance's feet. When it's like this between them she forgets his humour, his gentle way with her, the lovely, out-of-the-blue things he says, and in remembering how she forgets she must change the way she's standing, because she sees some of the anger go out of him.

'Michelle?'

In the shop, the man is ordering at the counter, looking up at the menu and talking. Like it's Alaska or something, he's wearing a red hat with ear flaps and a big black jacket.

More than any of the other shitty things, it's hunger that starts Michelle crying.

Lance holds back for a second and then opens his arms. She walks in between his feet. 'I'm hungry,' she says.

He holds her around the shoulders and then lets his arms slide down her back. He's really good at hugging, pulling her in and up a little, taking some of the weight out of her feet.

'The money belonged to one of the deli ladies,' he says, talking with his chin in her hair. 'She didn't want to press charges, but Jenna wanted me fired.'

Michelle's turned her head towards the shop, but is still pressed into Lance. The man's still ordering, talking up at the big menu, while bearded Den moves his pen across a pad on the counter. 'I got fired too. Mrs Watson took the money but said I couldn't stay on.'

'Did you tell her about a baby?'

'She got real angry—I didn't get a chance. Her husband started on me too.'

Now the man in the hat has sat on the low bench thing beneath a fish-species poster, looking at a cell phone.

Asking about her pub smell, Lance says, 'So did they pay you?'

'Making up that smoke I found two dollars in the couch. I gambled it up to eight and got a beer.'

'The Golden Arm,' goes Lance. 'Should've kept gambling.'

In the shop, Den's standing on a stepladder, using a rag against something on the blackboard.

'Did you get paid?' says Michelle.

'My last pay's Tuesday, minus the fifty. Jenna was a bitch, but not as much of a bitch as I expected.'

'What will we tell the PM?' Michelle tips back from Lance, wanting to see him laugh but also wanting to hold off talking about the power.

'Power's out, nothing in the fridge. Jacinda, we might have to cook your cat.'

'On, like, a camp stove.'

'Jacinda, we'll need you to bring your own camp stove.'

The good thing between them has returned and feeling good about that Michelle tickles her hands up Lance's cold sides, lighting his face in the same way Matador lit with that big win.

'You'd need a tin bucket to really do the job,' says Lance.

'A primus,' she says, 'a Bunsen burner.'

'Carrots, onions.'

'What do you call it? Stock.'

'Campbell's stock. Mmm, those cans of Campbell's beef stew.'

'With garlic bread, two big bottles of Steinlager and two litres of chocolate ice cream.'

'Cigarettes from a fresh pack.'

A bus passes. As if it's a threat, Lance holds her tight. 'I'm so hungry,' he says when its quieter again, and she knows he's feeling okay—later no doubt he'll start into some serious worrying—because he's started shivering, his teeth rattling around in his head, the anger in him spilled out all over the footpath. 'What's Den cooking?'

'Den cooks everything.'

To keep warm they're back to hugging, but both are squinting at Den's menu where steam creeps down the front window. You can still see in, though, and now the man on the bench sits forward and, like it's a crown, carefully takes off his hat, and straightaway, by the haircut, Michelle knows.

'Lance.'

'I'd get that King burger and—'

'*Lance.*'

Lance agreed to follow the man, but no more. 'We're unarmed,' he'd said. 'I don't know kung fu. This isn't TV, Michelle. What would we even do?'

One shop down, they're on a wooden seat beside a rubbish bin. They can still see Den's, but not what's happening inside.

'If he comes out and gets into a car, well, that's it,' says Lance, talking through his teeth that are still chattering.

Michelle looks around at the nearby cars. The sun's gone, deepening the sky's blue.

'We put a tail on, we don't do more than that,' goes Lance, then he dips his misshapen nose into the smock's V.

Cold off the seat spreads up Michelle's back. As if he's psychic, Lance gets closer and side-hugs her with his thin arm. Stomping on that empty cask the other night is about as violent as he gets.

Michelle clears the last taste of beer from her mouth and swallows. But what are they going to do? Go home? You can't eat cold and dark. You can't cook that empty can of fly spray into some delicious pie.

'There,' says Lance. 'Here, shit.'

Walking quickly, the man's already past, heading down the middle of the footpath with two plastic bags full of parcels. Lance moves and so does Michelle, up and away from the seat, up, away and following.

Out from under the last shop's eave, the man passes the bus from before that's taking on passengers. Jog-walking, Michelle goes, 'He must live close. Doesn't look like he's driving.'

There's the food smell and the low-hanging stink from the bus and she and Lance lead with their skinny shoulders, arrowing through the bus people. Ahead the man turns off the footpath, rounding the brown fence and shrubs planted in woodchips that mark the start of the playground. Down there are sports fields and the old skateboard bowls and when Michelle and Lance go around the fence that's the direction the man's headed—down a grass bank, towards the boggy-looking soccer field.

'Heading to one of those houses?' goes Lance.

Because beyond the skateboard area there's a longer, gentler bank, trees, and then a road of large houses set among tall trees, set up there with views of the tips of the city's tall buildings, the harbour and the peninsula which, in parts, the sun's still kissing.

Michelle remembers a teacher telling them once that after a certain amount of time without food your body will start feeding on its own muscle, will start eating itself.

The bottom of the bank comes fast and Michelle has to work to find her feet, while Lance hot-steps in the mud, basically going backwards, worried for some reason about keeping his shitty shoes clean. They're weak and slow—probably their bodies have already started on their muscle—while ahead this bull charges off with his dinner.

Behind her a bit, Lance says, 'I don't know, Michelle.'

It's the same scared voice that stopped her gambling those big wins. It's the same scared voice that stops her doing anything.

RUN. It isn't something she's done for a while and it takes a bit to get her arms right with her legs. Plus, she's looking for a weapon. But there's just the soccer field—grass, mud and lots of dirty little bits of blue-and-red electrical tape the players must use on their boots. Closing now on the hat and the cheerfully swinging food, the question now is has she got the right man? He turns his head slightly, the way you do when you've heard something and are thinking to stop and look properly. There *was* a moment outside Den's when she thought it was him, the man, he who now stops, turns, and faces her, the food dangling there like scales.

Eating chips, they're sat back on the duvet they pushed to the head of their bed, making room for the food. The wontons are gone, so is the fish. Less than half a hot dog nests in the chips. The curtains are half open, the room lit weirdly by the streetlight.

Lance eats more chips, food juice glistening on his chin.

By Michelle's bare right foot—her wet socks and grassy shoes are in the hall—there's a last unopened parcel. She moves her foot, brushing the grease-patterned paper.

'Hope it's not spring rolls,' goes Lance.

'Or battered sausages,' says Michelle.

What they're both hoping, but are too afraid to say in case they jinx it, is that the last parcel is dessert: doughnuts, or at least pineapple rings.

Michelle knows Lance's waiting for her. When they open the parcel is her decision. She did the thing that got the food. She puts in two more chips. Having absorbed the temperature of the room they're almost totally cold. Michelle's cooling down too. Soon they'll have to get under the duvet. The last thing to look forward to is this little parcel.

'Crab sticks,' goes Michelle, trying to hold the fun they've been having. 'Anything but crab sticks.'

Whacking with her arms so the food bags got free, she'd made a jumping tackle thing. Easily, the man went back and under her, so that it was like she'd jumped into the top of a mattress stood on one end. Getting up fast, not looking, she grabbed the bags and ran. Soon, Lance was running with her.

'And that was it,' Michelle says, like what she'd done—an assault, a robbery—was only a little more than nothing.

'Eh?' says Lance, taking more chips.

She doesn't explain and in a plain, almost sad voice, Lance says, 'Wish we had tomato sauce.'

When they first got home they'd been hysterical. Good hysterical. High, like with weed or a big win on Matador. They'd hugged, they'd kissed, they'd pinballed around the room. Then Lance made this big production of laying all the parcels on the bed. And something about the way he did it—like the parcels were museum antiques or something—got Michelle laughing. *Really* laughing. Like her ribs were going to break. And it—her hysteria—only increased when he opened the first two parcels, picking little holes in the paper and peering through, feeling around with his finger, making these game show type announcements. 'Wontons—won't you come on down!'

Michelle thought she was going to swallow her tongue. Or faint. The room was cold, but she was warm from running and there was all this food and her stomach was flip-flopping around like it was trying to get outside her skin and get started eating even before her mouth. And that thought—how hungry she was and how much food they had—made her laugh even harder.

'Hot dogs, ladies and gentlemen, meat on a stick!'

That bit caused her to collapse onto the floor. After a moment Lance joined her there, clutching four hot dogs in one hand, holding them like they were flowers.

Lance takes a chip. Until now he's been taking at least two. The world's coming back. All the shit they're in. Did she hurt the man? Will he call the cops? Sometime soon is someone going to be knocking on their door? Lance will find out they attacked the wrong man. Lance will leave her. The rent, the trouble at Mrs Watson's, the power . . .

But she got them food. They're not hungry anymore. *She* solved that problem.

Cold fat releases as she brings her back teeth down on another chip. The way she wishes she could redo a losing gamble, Michelle wishes she could go back in time—about fifteen minutes—to when they were really eating. They'd got onto the bed. Still with all four hot dogs, Lance had made his eyes wide—asking permission—and then, when she nodded, bitten the sauced tip off the longest dog. Chewing, swallowing, 'Oh,' he'd said, and then, no longer pretending, '*oh*.'

Watching, Michelle went hard at a wonton. Parts exploding both inside and outside her mouth—the crunchy batter breaking and then starting to dissolve as her tongue found the nest of salty meat. 'God,' she said.

Then she gave Lance a wonton and he gave her a hot dog. She bit off the sauce part, sending the sausage back to wait for processing while she finished the first wonton and picked up a second.

'Fish?' said Lance.

He'd already eaten one whole dog and then somehow fitted a wonton in. Breathing hard through his nose, still holding two hot dogs, he then took up a fillet of fish, gave it to Michelle while using his own fillet to encourage her to put the fourth—and final—wonton into his mouth.

Now Lance picks a chip, looking at it like he's going to say something she doesn't want to hear. But then he just puts it in and chews.

Is he going to judge her now? *After* he's eaten? So they took dinner from some dad walking back to a lounge full of his hungry family. But who'd needed it more? And if they didn't take it, who was coming to help them? The PM? Mrs Watson? The sweary guy behind her at the pub? Michelle eats more chips.

In the middle of her Matador session she got three nines. Gambled once, twice, three times, four, and then—BLACK, WINNER!—a fifth time and 15 credits became 480.

She feels for Lance's hand and holds it. Maybe instead of robbing the BP, they need to solve the electricity problem by—

'What are you thinking?' goes Lance.

Going down to the Octagon and watching an ATM. When someone takes out money, we follow—like we followed the man—and then . . .

She tips forward and takes up the parcel. It's lighter than a parcel of socks. 'Lance?' she says.

He stays quiet.

'Lance?'

'Yeah?' he says, after another moment.

Malcolm

It's been raining and the ditch to the side of the gravel track is muddy and puddled. Malcolm's wearing gumboots and green-and-blue overalls and now he sits and heels himself, feet first, down the bank, into a puddle.

'Puddle,' he says, stomping.

I crouch to be close in case of a problem, looking up and down the track. This place is popular with dog-walkers and, probably because of my own fear, I'm scared of dogs coming in fast and scaring Malcolm (or worse) with big teeth and jaws.

He dips the rice-cracker he's holding into puddle-water and takes a bite.

'Uh uh, no,' I say.

He chews, looking at me, and feints to dip again.

'C'mon,' I say. 'Not that. No, Malcolm.'

He stops—on his terms—and climbs up the bank where he kicks into the gravel, squats to finger it, then stands and says, 'Run, Daddy.'

My knees are old. These days in order to keep the weight out of them I mince rather than run. So, that's what I do, mince up the path, and that's more than enough for Malcolm who, getting going, getting his little arms working, runs, smiling up at me.

'Daddy's running.'

'I am,' I say, winding my own arms and gaping comically.

'Stop,' he says, so I do. 'Go,' he says, so I do.

And in this way, we get past the soccer field that makes the other side of the track and up to a place where there's a two-metre drop to the Kaikorai stream, where black water falls, making a white mat of bubbles.

'Blankie,' says Malcolm.

'It's back in the car, old mate,' I say. 'Blankie's in the car.'

Crouched again, I've got him between my knees with my hands around his stomach which goes out and in with his breath.

'Like blankie,' he says pointing, and I see what he means. The bubbling white water, the form of it, looks like his comforter.

'Yes,' I say, 'it is like blankie.'

Knowing this already, he doesn't respond.

He's twenty-seven months, and wears pull-ups for active boys weighing between thirteen and eighteen kilograms. He's into baked beans, gurnard, plates of oven fries, ice cream and dancing. He dances in our bedroom and the lounge, he dances with my old tennis racquet, checking his moves in the reflection made in our sliding doors, he strums and bobs and shifts from one foot to the other. Or for a whole song he'll just jump. Jump, play his guitar, hiccup and laugh.

Back where our car is parked, past the soccer field, there is the sound of car doors shutting.

'What's that noise?' says Malcolm.

'A car,' I say, picking up a small stone and lobbing it into the water. 'Plop,' I say, close to his ear.

But he's watching the car park. Two people stand by an old ute. A white dog sits by a rubbish bin.

'C'mon,' I say, 'let's run.'

I start to wheel away, but Malcolm, though he's standing, is still facing the dog and the people.

I'm in shorts, but also a puffer jacket. Malcolm is in a pirate's hat—the shape of Napoleon's—with a lamb's wool tunic over his overalls. Size-wise, he's on the seventy-fifth percentile. I was always small. At Otago Boys' High, I was puny with an oversized head and ears that stuck out. Occasionally I was bullied.

The occasion I remember clearest was at lunch during a summer inter-school. I played tennis and was sitting opposite a popular boy who, in the fifth form, was already an all-rounder in the First XI. We were at big tables, eating rolls filled with lettuce, hardboiled eggs and ham, and drinking from cardboard containers of Just Juice.

'Fucking look at this,' the all-rounder said, nudging the boy beside him, and pointing to me in my pastel-and-white tennis polo. 'Look at his fucking arms. How can he get the ball over the net?'

Chewing, the other boy nodded but stayed quiet.

Maybe it was his mate's lack of interest that made the all-rounder mad. 'Ethiopian,' he said, glaring. 'Fucking little Ethi.'

He was tall and broad with a tanned face and a long fringe and for the rest of the meal he glared and sniggered and kicked me under the table. Actually, I don't remember that. And I don't even know if he called me 'Ethi'. But this was the Eighties—the famines were on TV—and I did get called that occasionally. No doubt we had to stay seated at those plastic trestle tables until a teacher said we could get up. Probably the all-rounder lost interest in me and my arms almost immediately. Maybe he stuffed around with his juice container, maybe he popped it with the heel of his hand or shot the sugary juice out of the straw. Maybe he talked about the state of the game they were playing. But, twenty-seven years later, I remember sitting there opposite him, so I must have been scared.

'Up,' says Malcolm, raising his arms, still watching the dog which is lean and fast and making crazy swoops over the soccer field. I pick him up and walk. He's got his legs each side of my hip and his left hand on my right shoulder and he pushes his face into the wind as though I'm a horse he's riding one-handed. I'm glad he's big. I don't want him to be a bully, but I don't want him scared. I want him to be open and strong and fast to laugh. I want him to be known for his loud shirts and loud laugh. I want him into eye-popping recreations like kite-surfing or base-jumping. I want him drumming in a rock band and driving a convertible. I want him to be one of those people you think about when they're not around—a person of such presence that, in wondering where they are, you also feel envy at those lucky enough to be near them.

He twists and looks back down the track. 'What's that?' he says.

I turn. Now the dog's in the ditch drinking. On the path above, there's a man in a woollen hat and a woman.

'A dog, a thirsty doggy,' I say, wanting to sound casual, wanting to be a father who can deal with dangerous dogs with a loud voice or a well-timed kick.

Malcolm swivels again and I bump his ear with my cheek. His ears are soft, but not squishy. The cartilage shape of them is firm but pliable, and the delicate edge is cool against my cheek.

Ahead, the bush closes a little on each side of the track. Further on, it opens again and up there is the woodchip pile I'm aiming for.

We go past some low hanging trees and I dip and dive him through the wet leaves.

'Aaar!' he says, giggling, 'good game!'

I turn to run him through the leaves again. The dog's gone back to blasting around the soccer field. The man is still on the path, while the woman's out on the field with a lead, yelling at the dog. 'Hooper, Hooper! Come!'

The dog doesn't respond, just keeps running. Probably they're trying to get it under control before coming too close to us.

Even with all the drinking I've done, all the late nights out, I've never been in a fight. Never stood up for myself or someone else, or broken up some beastly act by, say, wrapping my arms around an offender, or crash-tackling some dick. I don't like violence. That's part of it. But the main part is cowardice. When a thing happens and the brain is charged with the chemical that imposes either fight or flight, I'll fly. But not if the thing was a person drowning in a river, or if a bedroom was burning up; then, I think, I'd go in. But not fighting. I mean, I'd defend

Malcolm, wouldn't I? Or Lisa, my wife? I'd fight then?

Malcolm's getting heavy, but I check back down the track before putting him down. 'Let's look for mushrooms,' I say.

He looks up at me. His eyes go wide and he flaps his mouth, 'A, a, a,' he says, sorting through the words in his brain. 'A mushroom hunt,' he goes.

'A mushroom hunt,' I confirm.

Ahead, I can see the woodchips. Beside the track are areas of mown, sloping grass. Beyond that, on our right, the council has planted toetoe and other natives on a hill that gets steep fast, while on the other side, between the track and stream, there's the grass, a picnic table and then some scruffy bush where we've found mushrooms before.

I look back, but the track's curved slightly and I can't see the people or the dog. I dangle my hand and Malcolm takes it. Earnestly, in a clear, wonderful voice, he says, 'It's a good walk.'

At his twenty-first, at his wedding, at his child's first birthday, on the day he buys his first house or makes a big impression in some big city, I want to be beside him, elegantly dressed, holding a glass of champagne, saying some wise and funny thing while his friends/lovers/wife/children smile and raise their drinks as I hug him and tell him I'm proud, that I can't love anything more than I love him.

We cross the grass and he leads me, ducking, into the bush which is dark and cool and where the sound of the stream is louder.

A year or more after that inter-school lunch, the all-rounder was driving the Northern motorway late at night with some of the other popular boys when he lost control of the car and hit and killed a woman whose own car had broken down. The all-rounder's brother had been a prefect and then maybe dux. His dad had a firm offering financial services for wealthy Dunedinites. After a short time, while he was away from school, there was a court appearance and after that the all-rounder was back and playing again for the First XI.

'Mushroom,' goes Malcolm.

I look. 'I think it's a bone. It's a similar colour, though, isn't it?'

Malcolm squats and prods. 'Bone,' he says.

I crouch and we investigate. 'Might be from a sheep.'

'Might be,' he says.

'Or a dog—a hyena,' I say, because it's a word he's enjoyed before.

But he doesn't say anything, just runs his fingers absently over the bone.

'Shall we go up to the woodchips?' I say.

He looks at me, light coming into his eyes. 'I like chips.' He throws his arms into the air with such gusto that his feet leave the ground and he rotates slightly on the spot.

Leading the way I go back out onto the grass. No sign of the dog or the people, but there is barking. I look at where I exited the bush, where Malcolm now comes, stumbling and then tripping and then standing. His pirate hat's fallen low over his eyes, but despite that he starts to walk, tipping his head right back to see.

'I'm sing you a song, Daddy,' he says.

I wait for him and adjust his hat. 'A song?'

'Yeah,' he says, nodding in his serious way, like it's something he's been thinking about for a long time.

'At the woodchips?' I say, taking his hand and heading towards the mound.

'Hmm.'

Again I look down the path, but now even the barking's stopped. Maybe the animal and its owners have gone back to the car.

There was my friend Rhys. Rhys killed himself. After university we flatted together in a shit-box at the Jervois Road end of John Street in Herne Bay. I was working in a factory, he was a junior pharmacist in Kingsland. After work, we'd lift weights at a Newton gym and then take benzodiazepine and drink wine cooler. On his OE he got into the medical heroin returned by families of people who'd been using the drug for relieving pain related to terminal cancer. He made it back to Auckland, but overdosed in his bathroom in a flat in West Auckland. Deregistered, he returned to the UK, where he overdosed again and died, aged twenty-five.

The woodchip pile makes a stage a metre off the ground. I'm sitting off to the side, looking at Malcolm who's up there with a toetoe stem. Now he squats, working his lower hand as though it's the strings of a double bass he's playing.

'Oh,' I say, 'yes.'

'Ooh ya,' he says, smiling and bobbing.

I applaud. 'Is that your song? Ooh ya?'

'Ooh ya,' he sings, 'ooh ya.'

What a scene. Framed by green trees and a clear sky,

golden hair curling beneath his skull and crossbones. In concentrating on getting his voice low or high, he sometimes forgets to play the toetoe, just stands tall and thrusts his heart forward, bellowing, and as long as I'm prepared to hoot and yell 'Bravo, encore, encore!' he's happy to set himself for another brief performance.

But then, beyond him, I see the couple. Because Malcolm's blocking some of the path, I can't see the dog, but when I move a bit I see it's close, white wolfish jaws so relaxed its teeth clatter lightly as it comes on, undulating.

'Malcolm,' I say, and straight onto the fear in my voice, he stops his song and reaches for me, but though I've said his name urgently, my feet are onions, and instead of standing and throwing him onto my shoulders, instead of preparing a defence, I sort of crawl forward and around the woodchips—at least I'm between him and the dog, the dog that's only ten metres away, eye to eye with a skinny, unshaven, forty-three-year-old.

'Hooper! Hooper!' goes the woman, 'Daddy,' says Malcolm, 'Hey,' says the male dog-walker, and so mine is the only brain not vocalising, instead it's got me elbows down in the path, my forehead gravel-bound, my bum raised, so what I am is a ramp for the animal to run and leap and hunt my son's throat. My brain—and what it's learnt of submitting before wild animals from Wilbur Smith novels and David Attenborough documentaries—supplicates my body before this scrawny dog that now skids in, lipping gravel onto my hands, but instead of fangs, or even hot breath, all I feel is a wet nose sniff-sniffing over my head.

And then a tongue in my ear. 'Yeah,' I say, to the gravel, 'yes,' and finally I reach back for Malcolm who must have already come off his stage, because he finds me first, setting his little hand on my back, and it's this contact that gets me looking up.

'It's okay, it's okay,' says the woman, who's standing there on the path, looking at me shyly, and here's the man, who, same as the dog, has a wrinkled face and a bulging right eye, and he says, 'Hooper likes children, he can't get enough of them,' and so I change from my submissive shape to a more standard, dog-patting crouch, while at the same time gathering Malcolm close, and, after a moment—the animal's dead-still, stunned maybe by the thing it had me do—I get back to being Dad, showing Malcolm where to scratch and which way to stroke the fur.

'Dog,' says Malcolm.

'Hooper,' I say, my voice sounding like it's coming through the radio. 'This is Hooper.'

The man—he seems the least thrown by my performance—nods at Malcolm. 'It's a good day for pirating.' But Malcolm's shy around men and after staring at him a moment he says, 'Up,' and so finally I pick him up, holding him, as Hooper—who's also come back to himself—licks the soles of Malcolm's gumboots.

'All right,' I say, raising my eyebrows at the couple, who move a little up the path but then stop and watch while Malcolm dangles his hand to Hooper's lapping tongue.

The woman looks at my dusty knees and nods.

I nod too. 'Bye, Hooper,' I say, and start walking back down the track.

In my arms, Malcolm turns and looks over my shoulder: maybe at the dog, maybe at the friendly man, maybe at the path that becomes a track that leads up to Brockville with its wind, views, bus stops and state houses.

Your son killing someone. Your son killing himself. Neither of those two outcomes would be good for a parent. But, inescapably, that's what I am now—a parent.

In summer, at the Logan Park courts, from age ten to sixteen, me and Dad used to play tennis after tea until it got so dark the ball would disappear when you hit it over the net. Dad, whose black beard has gone totally silver, who, when he was my age, was divorced and doing the Coast to Coast every year while his own parents, now dead, were both, I don't know, playing five hundred with their cobbers, camping in their huge, pre-World War II tent, or having their dinner in front of the TV while Tom Bradley read the news.

When Dad was my age now, I was fourteen. I hadn't yet left that John Street flat, hadn't yet left Rhys there with all his pills and moved to stay with Grandad in Christchurch, where, lonely and depressed, and feeling under pressure to get my own OE started, I forged Grandad's name on one of his cheques, banked five thousand of his dollars and disappeared to Perth.

I put Malcolm down, but hold his hand. What we'll do is go and buy a popsicle from the Four Square on Kaikorai Valley Road. He'll eat his and then get little bites from mine and then we'll do something with the sticks—draw on faces or use a rubber band to make aeroplanes.

Adult life: for Malcolm, it's just a series of days and

nights away. And right now is a Sunday, in February 2017, and he's two years and three months old. At the moment he's getting used to a new timetable of daycare, he's learnt to get in and out of his car seat on his own, he can pull his trousers up but only at the front, he doesn't know the vacant feeling you get from benzos, he doesn't know about cigarettes or impotence, he doesn't know that the night before I was flying out to Perth with my stolen money I stayed with Rhys and we got drunk, and in the morning I woke up on his kitchen floor, looking at the yolk, white and shell of an egg Rhys had dropped when he was preparing to cook me one of his famous fried-egg and melted cheese sandwiches.

'We'll get a popsicle, eh?' I say.

'I like popsicles,' he says.

'Popsicle,' I say, aware that since the thing with the dog my voice has not come right.

'Run, Daddy,' he says.

And so we run. Him on the gravel, me, still protecting my knees, on the grass, down towards where his blankie will always be trapped in the back flow caused by water falling.

Being Sonya

Sonya's pregnant—that's what she told Ian anyway—but it's slow being home all day, so she's started taking the Tramadol prescribed following his accident. Now it's mid-morning and she swallows one of the yellow/green capsules with the last of her coffee.

Along with her mug there are a few dishes left from breakfast and she runs hot water in the sink, adds detergent, and gets in with the long-handled brush. The remains of Ian's bircher—since finding out, he's cut back on sugar and they've started walking more. She finishes, leaving the dishes draining in the low winter sun.

Out there is a gully of native bush and then two brick houses at the end of a cul-de-sac. Along from the cul-de-sac is a playground Sonya's been walking to every morning, waiting on her high. Drying her hands, she goes through their small rented villa. Updated bathroom, updated open-plan kitchen/living area, while the rest of the house is pretty much just two high-ceilinged bedrooms off the hallway.

Down the hall and out the front door in Ian's puffer jacket, up concrete steps to the footpath. No cars or people. Faintly, from the direction of Highgate, a siren. From here the view is of harbour, stadium and the tall beige buildings around the hospital. Tiny cars wheel the peninsula road.

Two tugs motor out of sight. Low light from a sun now buried under grey. Work thinks she had a miscarriage. She described it in her email as traumatic both physically and psychologically. Subject line: Indefinite Leave Required. She starts walking. Across the road, behind netting, chickens move about.

Last night Ian asked, 'When will you get bigger?'

They were on the couch and before she could answer, he'd ducked his smiling face to her belly, putting his ear in as if listening for a heart.

Lovely Ian. Hard-working, honest and determined to be a really good dad. She hadn't wanted to tell him she couldn't face going to work, that she couldn't cope. Lies had been such a big part of her twenties and so here she is, comfortable for now in the gentle, harmless section of her deceit.

But a knife-man couldn't make her take another call. The Dunedin branch of the ACC call centre. Tradies shouting about uncovered shoulder injuries, callers with their Sensitive Claim letters asking how the government can help them through. Upbeat team-leaders in sweat-stained shirts. Graduates saving for their OE. Nervy, worn-out mums returning to the workforce. Sonya used to throw up before shifts; she'd started hanging up on callers. No way is she going back.

Walking along the road, watching her shoes rise and fall, not high yet, but aware it won't be long. A man up a ladder, preparing a house for paint. The shriek of the tool he's using. More sirens—multiple vehicles?—closer and louder. When she gets home she'll put a beer in the freezer with a glass, have a long, ultra-hot shower and then sit on the couch drinking. Tramadol brings delicious thirst. Also, nausea and itching. Best is the euphoria. Just *being* Sonya, it feels so good. What a good catch she's become. The nice feeling vacuuming puts in her arm muscles. And the other day, working her homemade herb butter under the skin of that chicken, coaxing it over the breast, down into its wing pits.

Cresting the hill, past the workman, past a gutter bulging with brown leaves big as dinner plates, past the big rocks placed to keep car-hoons off the playground, and onto the playground itself. Swings, two old-fashioned see-saws, red monkey bars.

'The best chicken ever!' was what Ian said about that bird.

Since she and Ian have been together her strengths have increased. Cooking, obviously, but also sticking to things—twelve months she was at ACC.

There's a grass bank before a narrow road that disappears into the town belt. She sits on a bench seat as two vans drive the curve of the broader main road. Beyond them is a soccer field, shrubs and then more of the town belt. Out of nowhere a man's walking a little dog.

'Hi,' he says.

Sonya sits forward on the seat with her hands on the cold wood as if in her mind is a plan to stand. 'Hi.'

He passes and she sits back. A red helicopter's out over the harbour.

Last night, sex made a good distraction from Ian's weight question. Instead of answering, she'd just changed her couch position and kissed him. Her orgasm was blunted a little by the Tramadol, or maybe it was Ian not being so determined—near where things got important, he'd eased, asking if what he was doing was okay, if it wasn't too rough.

The obvious way out of the pregnancy is to invent a miscarriage. But how about getting pregnant? There was no contraception last night. Why would there be? Clearly Ian's keen. Clearly he's desperate to get down to BabyMart or wherever and start spending. Some of the maths wouldn't make sense, but she could blur that easily enough. She's so decisive when it comes to lying.

Interrupting her thoughts, timing their arrival with her first awareness of the drug, three police cars come from three different directions, parking in a place where buses turn at the bottom of the bank. Policemen get out quickly from two cars, go to the window of the third, then return to their own vehicles and drive off in different directions. The third car stays, the lights on its roof silently rippling.

Sonya watches. Wouldn't very dry champagne be nice? With Ian, yes. She genuinely wishes he was here. And feeling so sure of that fact makes it even more pleasurable to imagine. He's fast with jokes in these situations. Physically he's nimble and strong, and with words he's the same. Lately—it's not something they've discussed—he's started wearing his hair back from his forehead. She'll ask him about it over dinner. It's the sort of thing around which he'll sling a good joke. She gives herself back to the surrounds, but it's hard to ignore the police car. The word 'sting' comes into her mind. Not as in wasp, but some sort of sneaky operation. She closes her eyes and sits right back, opening them on seagulls—black ticks—soaring.

There with them is a disk of moon. Pocked in the same way fat pocks salami, while the moon would be closest to the colour of that fat. She loves Ian and wants to be with him. Well, a version of herself is in love, and wants to stay that way. To buy a house. To have a child—or children, she'll make ham sandwiches, they'll all come here to play and picnic—with him. She scratches her hand and then reaches up under the breast of his jacket to scratch around the edge of her bra. To get older and older in his company.

Get pregnant, then? Maybe the reason she's always parking herself here is some kind of sign. Or maybe what she's doing with this lie is breaking them up? She did way worse that time with Gregor. Starting the lie off when they were living in Te Anau and really twisting the knife after he'd covered the cost of their move to Tauranga.

'New Zealand,' she says, thinking about the length of two islands while watching the police car, which, lights included, is now totally idle.

What could be going on around this nice neighbourhood?

'Someone left their hair dryer on,' she says, looking over her shoulder to see if anyone's caught the joke.

But there's no one except the cold wind in the grass and a selection of daisies plus those yellow ones that aren't buttercups. Could she bouquet them up for Ian? The thought is dismissed. She's confident in overseeing the addling impact of Tramadol. No way is she one of those smelly druggie types you see around.

*

Home. Ah, home. Down the concrete steps and through the front door. Straight from the pantry to the freezer with the beer and then into the bathroom where she undresses, folding each item onto the toilet seat while steam fills the room, sucking fast through the open window.

She hasn't really told Ian much about her twenties. *I drank too much, moving from one town to the other. I had a lot of relationships with unsuitable people.* That's as detailed as it got. Violence happened back then, though. Against her, and by her.

Acting on that memory—having just stood under the water until now—she sets to with Ian's shower brush. Scouring her legs, reaching back over each shoulder to go up and down over her lumbar area. Then, choking it below the neck, she gets about her arms. Finished, her skin crimson with the attention, she goes back to hanging under the hot water like a figure from a mobile.

Mum's to blame. Dying, you know, in my late teens. It left my boat a little rudderless. How many conversations in pubs and bars did she insert that into? 'Rudderless'. A way to get *in.* A way of letting another person know she wasn't in control, that she was up for anything. That word and her smile, the way she could sparkle her eyes—people were so easily convinced they mattered!

'Your eyes,' Ian would say. 'Jesus, they detonate.'

Noise comes from one of the bedrooms. Wind under the iron roof. Ian's been up there with rat traps. She flicks the shower dial into cold and, raising her arms, lets the cold cross her armpits. Then she turns slowly, stops, and turns again, letting every part of her taste. Ian introduced her—a blast of cold after the heat. 'Brings you alive,' he'd say, sliding soapy hands over her waist.

Another thing that turns him on is when his financial advisor sends details about his portfolio. Graphs inserted into quarterly reports. Heavy, insistent language about yields and profits. He hasn't got much in there yet, but since Sonya's known him it's almost doubled. He's good with money. He works hard. Not that he's National or Act—he cares about people, he's against inequality, also in the mail they get information about a boy in Bangladesh he's been supporting since before Sonya.

'I just want to be the best version of myself,' he said once, 'which is where you come in.'

Sonya gets out of the shower. With his soft, camel-coloured towel she pats at her skin. Why didn't she just tell him she couldn't handle the call centre? He'd have understood. Probably he would've been encouraging. Probably some sort of relationship-building interaction might have taken place.

Outside are more sirens and then another round of the noise. A rattling—has a bird got into one of the bedrooms? Is Ian home? Ian with his wonderfully mean mouth—the only tough part of him. That would be a bind—him coming in, her having beer. Defend drinking while pregnant or admit to lying . . . But she could handle it. What did someone say? She was both snake and charmer.

Rising to full height, she wraps herself in the towel and goes into the hall. 'Ian?'

The tone of her voice—a little panicked—makes her smile.

'Ian?'

This time it comes out better, but there's no response. Their bedroom's cold and she needs to make the bed. No Ian, though. She goes back into the hall where a draught's at her heels. Into the spare bedroom. Ian's exercycle and the poster of the man with a beard standing beside an old-fashioned saw. Nothing else in here but the cold wooden floor. Courtesy of Tramadol there's a little seasickness, but mostly Sonya feels wonderful.

'Beer o'clock,' she tells the sawyer.

Sitting on the couch, pouring beer into the frosty glass, looking up to see a kererū, wings tucked, missiling past. Raising her glass to the bird, she lets the nearly frozen liquid slide into her mouth, holds it a moment exploring—citrus against malt—and then swallows. And right then, as the beer goes down, footsteps.

'Ian?'

She thinks of where she could hide the glass, but then a woman's there, looking.

Big nostrils. Very dirty shoes. A straight back.

There's quiet as they look at each other. Then Sonya goes, 'Hi?' at the same time the woman goes, 'Is this your house?'

'Umm, yeah?'

Confused, Sonya's thinking back to last night/this morning, trying to locate memories of Ian saying something that might explain a visitor. Instead what she remembers is her old life. It was chaotic like this—random people, scary people. Not that this woman's scary. Mid-fifties and, other than the shoes, well-dressed. Tidy trousers, a fitted jersey—clothes you might see on one of the golf courses around here.

Sonya stands with her beer. It's okay, this interruption. The past has taught her she can handle pretty much anything. It would be better to be dressed, though. 'Are you here for Ian?'

Golf-lady's big boned, but Sonya would be stronger—she's sure of that. Ha! If it comes down to anything, she won't be worried.

As if sensing something's relaxed in Sonya, the woman exhales, and like it's the punchline of some weird knock-knock joke, goes, 'Ian? Ian who? Is this his house?'

Thinking of another explanation for her presence, Sonya uses a harder voice, 'Why are you here?'

Because ACC employs investigators. Occasionally you got calls from people keen on dobbing in clients they thought were rorting the system. The neighbour with the 'bad back' seen painting his roof. The hairdresser with RSI doing cuts in her kitchen. Stuff like that. Would work deploy someone to verify her miscarriage? You couldn't put anything past the Corporation.

But the woman's ignoring Sonya. She's stepped away to look around. The wood burner, the antique fire tools hung there. Neatly stacked wood. Framed photos on the fireplace of Ian and Sonya holidaying on Banks Peninsula.

'I used to live here,' goes the woman.

Lightness returns and Sonya takes a good long drink. It's her house after all. 'And you've still got a key?'

The woman ignores the sarcasm. 'With my husband. With our three-year-old.'

'Hmm.'

'The door *was* open,' goes the woman, seeming to notice the beer for the first time, looking at Sonya a certain way.

'And what? You walk into any old house where a door's open?'

Sonya says it meanly. Then straightaway, embarrassed—Ian, no doubt, would have been overly polite, already he would have made coffee and shown her the different rooms, asking after their history—she starts to follow with something about getting dressed, but like Sonya will know exactly what she's talking about, the woman, firming even further through the back, looking like this is what she's here to say, says, 'Since the diagnosis, I've dispensed with certain courtesies.'

'Sorry? I just—' Sonya points at the bathroom, as if the woman will know that's where her clothes are folded.

'Our son died in that room you do your exercising.'

'Ian, umm—'

'He suffocated.'

'Suffocated?'

The woman nods. Then gestures at her chest, and as if now listing things that kill, says, 'Cancer. What I seem to be doing is going around the important places.'

'Shit,' says Sonya.

Smiling, the woman stays quiet, just raises her arms and then lets them flop to her side as if she couldn't have chosen a better word herself.

'We had bean bags.'

Sonya's dressed. They're both on the couch. Holding a

glass of beer, the woman's using it and her other hand to frame part of the carpet.

'Two of them, right there. My husband bought more beads for one—to fatten it out. Fatten it out . . . The things you remember.'

Sonya drinks. 'Mmm.'

They don't know each other's names. The woman seems above that. She's here for her own thing. 'So, he got this big plastic bag of beads and filled the bean bag, but the polystyrene things got all over the place, and by the time we hoovered them up, our son had taken the empty plastic bag into that front room of yours.'

Sonya finishes her beer. 'God.'

A dead boy in there. The face. Little breath drops on the underside of the plastic. Like the plastic was a wet windshield the boy was staring through. The inclination to say something tender crosses, but worried it won't come out properly, Sonya bites it back.

Then there's sustained knocking at the front door.

Two policemen, stance and faces familiar from the playground.

'Hello,' one says.

Sonya is liquid honey. 'Aren't you supposed to say something like "Morning, ma'am"?'

They shift a little and look past her.

Smiling and then shooting her chin as if to reset a more attentive, serious mode, Sonya says, 'Sorry.'

'You live here with—'

'Ian, Ian Cruickshank, the King of Scotland.'

'Rent or own?'

'We just bought it!'

The men nod and smile a little—they too can relate to the first rung of the property ladder. The shorter one's been taking notes and now, while the taller one scrutinises the villa's brand-new guttering, he clears his throat.

'A woman's been entering properties in the neighbourhood. We're concerned there may be a link to an early-morning attack at a local dairy. Have you seen or heard anything suspicious?'

Sonya pretends to think a moment, raising her hand to her chin as if putting in real effort. 'No,' she says, shaking her head slowly. Then, part of the investigation team, 'What transpired at the dairy?'

'Violence,' goes the taller of the two. In the way his nose attaches to his face, Sonya remembers Gregor.

'Two-way violence,' continues the other policeman.

Widening her eyes, Sonya brings her hands down to encircle the place her fake baby is growing. 'The *state* of this world,' she says.

Getting an idea of her condition, or maybe just enjoying the way she's supplicating herself, the men—in their marvellous costumes—stand a little prouder. The note-taker glances side to side as if checking for attackers, and the taller one says, 'One one one,' using tone to remind her it's a lesson he knows she knows, but that, judging by her pretty face and pleasing little abode, it's probably a lesson she hasn't needed to revise recently.

'We didn't get your name.'

Sonya curtsies her way back into the house. 'Alice

Murray.'

'Morning then, Alice,' says the tall one, making a flirty salute.

Returning his smile, Sonya carefully closes the door on them. The house is dead quiet. The smell of her shower—her squeaky-clean body—still fills the hall.

'Hello?' she says.

Nothing. Some of the beautiful feeling fades. '*Hi*?'

What would robbers take from a dairy? Cigarettes, cigarettes, more cigarettes.

The lounge is empty. So too the kitchen, just a fly on the window above the sink. Lies were made for the police, but you don't want some crazy bitch sneaking around. The combination of these thoughts makes her want a cigarette—another beer too—and so she leans down into the pantry, pulling one from its green box.

The woman will be in the sawyer's room. The information arrives so clearly—as if a plane drags it on a banner across the sky—that Sonya's high spikes, and in one smooth motion she stands, unscrews the beer cap, flicks it hard in the direction of the fly, and takes a long pull. Beer bubbles close on her nostrils. Something outside catches her eye, but when she turns towards the window it's gone.

The house stays quiet. 'Got any smokes?' goes Sonya.

Nothing.

She opens the drawer they keep cooking tools in. Kitchen scissors, the whisk, Ian's Akaroa corkscrew. In the case of a home invasion what implement would you grab? Gregor loved this game. *It's winter. You're locked out of your flat and have to spend the night in the car port. What two things from your room would you most want?*

With a meat hammer in one hand and the beer in the other, Sonya goes back through the house.

'You're suffocating me!' shouts Sonya.

Arms crossed, Ian stands with his back to the kitchen sink. There's a hint of something—fear? misery?—in his voice, but mostly, so far anyway, he's staying in control, as again he calmly demands, 'Are you pregnant?'

On the bench in front of Sonya, salt crystals glisten on a fist-sized piece of rib-eye. A firm head of emerald-green broccoli lies beside two shallots she was going to use for the pepper sauce. Behind her, in the fan oven, a potato pie bubbles.

'You're an arsehole, Ian.'

'I'm the arsehole?'

She swivels, holding out her hands. 'Oh, yeah, really nice. Call me an arsehole while I'm cooking all this?'

'Where's my Tramadol?'

Shooting off these black-and-white questions since he got home. Tramadol, the pregnancy—cunning Ian got suspicious and called ACC.

'Who're you ringing next? My GP? I'm sure she'll let you see my blood tests.'

If she can draw him into another sort of argument—about his breach of her privacy—and turn herself into a victim, maybe the guilt will soften him enough for her to reboard his plane. Later she can circle back to what work told him, fanning up a whole new array of lies.

But Ian's holding firm. 'What about that bag of bottles?'

'What beer bottles?'

'Beer bottles? I didn't say beer bottles.'

Sonya slams the meat with the flat of her hand. A shallot rolls off the bench and bounces, ending up between his feet. 'What is this? The cryptic fucking crossword?'

His face. Looking at her like she's made of that blue cheese he hated—over-ripe stuff they laughed about on their little trip through Ōamaru that time.

Now his mean mouth screws into a smile. 'Did you think you'd totally blinded me?'

She scratches back behind her ear down her neck, then claws between her eyes. With Gregor she left in the middle of the night. His station wagon, money card and warmest hoodie. The stuff they'd been into—no way was Gregor calling the cops.

'Haven't heard you complaining,' she mumbles, trying to swallow the words back even as they come out, because really, she has no clue what she means, let alone how it will help. Probably what she's meaning is the different ways she's let him use her body. Her body, his chopping board. Her body, his Pyrex oven dish containing potato pie. His shallots. His shallow frying pan behind her on the stove top. His olive oil. If he makes her leave, she'll have clothes and some toiletries.

Sadly, with her fingertips, she reshapes the beef. 'I'll just chuck this in the bin then.'

But he doesn't react to her sulky tone. Just stares, standing there in his cherry and sky-blue striped business shirt. Sleeves rolled halfway up his forearms.

'I've always hated your work shirts. That one looks like

toothpaste.'

She makes it—despising his work-wear—a confession. As if it's something she *has* kept from him, but is now—with this other stuff swirling—willing to confess to. In other words, yes, she has deceitful traits, but they're minor, they're nothing like what he's charging her with.

All he does is sigh.

Not used to exasperating him, she lets fly. 'What sort of fuckhead rings their partner's work, fishing for information?'

The energy she puts into the question immediately burns through her anger and right away she's thinking about cities and towns she hasn't lived in. Inland ones, coastal ones. Small is better. Places she'll be new and exotic—a beautiful bird resting. Fairlie, Waihi, Temuka . . .

'Who lies about having a baby?'

They've lived together three months, but now he's totally unfamiliar. His voice, tone, even his stance. And now, cracking, he starts crying. 'I even texted Dad—told him I had big news.'

Sloppy. Since the intruder. Piggy-backing the morning Tramadol with an afternoon hit. Drinking too much. The empties by the mailbox—she'd forgotten to walk them over to the bin at the park.

Ian moves past her. The smell of his workplace, deodorant, printing paper, some musky oiliness Sonya's always associated with male scalps. She considers hysteria. She considers pivoting towards a larger lie. She considers framing a full confession inside a grander, more dramatic truth.

Grabbing the broccoli, holding it like a microphone, she says, 'Ian, don't leave. I love you.'

Many years later Sonya is shopping at the supermarket on Highgate, not far from the house she shared with Ian. She's convinced she's shrunk, though her doctor tells her she's the same height she's always been. Maybe it's your posture, he says, but there's *nothing* wrong with her posture. Looking at the bucket of free fruit parents give kids to keep them quiet, Sonya again checks on her money card. She's forgotten the shopping list—her short-term memory is another complaint—but it's icy out there. No way is she scrabbling back up the hill.

'I'll figure it out, I'll freestyle,' she says in a hard sort of voice, a voice asking for response. But people—the teenager stacking celery, the bearded young man selecting bananas—don't look over, let alone say anything.

A small number of groceries looks bad in a big trolley, so she's towing a basket on a plastic leash. Tinted glasses, an old knee-length coat, her long glossy hair in an ugly bun, she loves it when people mistake her for sixty or whatever, for someone pension-age. Loves the indignation she's able to strike back with. It's a trap, she supposes, she's still able to set.

Passing through PRODUCE, she aims at FISH.

Not that she can't still look good. Friday nights she transforms. Careful make-up, arranging and then rearranging her few good clothes, then a taxi down to one of the Octagon pubs to watch and wait.

'Hello?' goes Sonya.

The fishmonger—bouncy looking, piercings—turns from what she's doing. 'Sorry?'

'Gurnard. A fillet, please.'

Sonya still tries to eat well. That's something she's carried over from Ian. Food was important to him and didn't she have a feeling for it! Following complicated recipes, shopping for good ingredients, thinking ahead in terms of *mise en place*.

The phrase—and the application of it to her old self—causes Sonya to bobble with pleasure and she sashays down the display. Whole monk fish, staring. Frozen sardines. Blue-cod wings. Fish stock, she thinks. Chowder. Her and Ian at Fleur's in Moeraki. Rabbits on that coastal track from where, at dusk, they watched penguins come ashore. The sunrise—him putting on her sweatshirt, going out to get coffee.

Ian. Cutting her off so coldly the night of the steak and potato pie. Asking her to leave in that ultra-formal way—like he was some earl and she an overstayer from a nearby estate, residing briefly on his holding.

Suddenly irritated, as if it was them who kicked her out, Sonya makes a dismissive gesture towards the sea creatures and asks loudly, 'It's fresh today, is it?'

'Sorry?' goes the girl, looking back over her shoulder.

'The fish. Did they bring it out of the ocean today?'

'It's all fresh,' goes the girl.

'That's not what I asked.'

The girl doesn't answer, just stands there wrapping the fish.

Trust issues, that's what Sonya has. A psychologist told

her. An addictions counsellor told her. Every fucker lining up to tell her.

Faking it, the girl now hands Sonya her dinner. 'Have a nice day.'

Sonya doesn't respond, just bends to put the parcel in her basket and goes deeper into the store.

MEAT now. The long shallow fridge of it. A red mattress of beef, lamb, offal. She stands, swaying, trying to remember what was on her shopping list, unaware she's got her hand over her throat, as though someone might leap out of CEREALS with a knife.

On her Octagon nights, she always arrives early to get a table, sipping a drink, smiling, making sure she's open to anyone who might think to join her. Nights pass and no one sits. Other nights a person might start with, 'Is this seat taken?' or 'Don't I know you from somewhere?'

Times are they'll get her a drink. Times are they'll have drugs to share.

'Times are . . .' says Sonya.

So masculine, a meat fridge. The urge is to climb in and snuggle with the different cuts. *Always seeking company in the wrong places!* Instead of bedding down she keeps herself moving, stopping at a display of precooked rice, staring at the different flavour options like they're book spines at the library.

Out at night, fishing, Sonya tells two stories. Ian/the intruder and Gregor. Other things have happened to her, but for whatever reason these are the memories she regurgitates. The details, the broader stuff, the tone in which she delivers the story, depend on who she's talking to. Certain types like meek and vulnerable. They want to hear she's suffered, they want to hear about *need*. For them then, in the case of her and Gregor, she switches roles.

'He stole my money card and car. He left me in the middle of the night.'

Other types—men, usually—love to hear about violence. They want to sit back from their drinks and gape at the things she's done. Later they'll lead her from the bar and into their bedrooms. There, hurting her, they'll think they're teaching her things about violence, domination and the power of money. So to hook these jerk-offs she makes up a horrible fight with the intruder. Hair-pulling, fingernails, blood.

And what they do to her doesn't matter. Once the trap's been sprung, Sonya's got guaranteed ways of making sure every transaction results in something coming her way.

Listening to the song over the supermarket speakers, she drifts down CEREAL. Stopping, she itches one shin and then the other. Light from above pools on the polished floor. Behind a fenced-off area—little cones, black-and-yellow rails—a staff member sweeps up rolled oats. A smiling mother with a baby in a backpack passes. Then two men.

Truth is, the intruder was squatting in the sawyer's room, her hands on the floor as if she was getting ready to tip forward onto her knees.

'He died right here.'

She wasn't crying, but her face—the way it was shaped—looked ready to go.

'The cops looking for you?' Sonya said.

'I doubt it,' said the woman, then stood in a business-like way, as if her visit was over, as if other houses needed haunting.

Enjoying the company, enjoying the faint feeling of danger, enjoying her second beer, Sonya had said, 'I can't wait to be a mother.'

The woman raised her arms over her head, taking a big breath. Then she dropped her arms and, like a swimmer warming herself for a race, started rotating them in circles—which was as close as they got to violence. When she smiled, her face became something beautiful and surprising, making what she said next an even harder punch.

'You can wait, all right. You're not the mothering type.'

So sure she was right about what she was saying. So light about it. Such a happy fact she was passing on. Of course she was right, but it cracked Sonya's shell to be seen so clearly.

Now leaving behind the different muesli options, Sonya circles a selection of pink lady-razors and enters WINE. And all of them—Gregor, Ian, the intruder—they're sucked out of a hole on her plane, because look at this! Like it's all been laid out for her! All the proud little bottles—labels front and centre—are watching, the supermarket music is her soundtrack, and Sonya, Sonya with her tight package of fish in her otherwise empty basket, is a glorious float at a street parade, she's a winning sailor on an America's Cup yacht, and any minute now she'll take off her dark glasses and raise her arms to the ticker tape and confetti.

Kid and the Tiger

Kid feels amazing, like angel's, nah, bat's wings are folded away in his hoodie. Swooping's what he'll do, swooping up and down over the zoo on this blue-sky day. Ever since they opened their lives to Jesus he's had all this . . . this—

'VROOM,' he says, gripping his hands like he's got the handles of a Harley, blatting towards Vanessa and Abraham, waving the tickets, saying, 'So, let's go look at what God made,' in a loud voice, sharing, in this way, His word, with some of the other families getting themselves organised near the ticket kiosks.

Kid's twenty-four, Vanessa's eighteen. Vanessa does long hours at Subway, while Kid looks after two-year-old Abraham. Kid and Vanessa met leading a party lifestyle in Hamilton—Vanessa had left high school, Kid was just out of prison—and over that time, Abraham happened. Then, three Saturdays back, Vanessa got talking to a man she was preparing a big order for. The next morning the man came to their unit and took them all to church. Since then, they've cut the drugs and drinking (mostly), married at the registry office (the fastest way), made an application to change their son's name (Shawn to Abraham) and switched to a Christian lifestyle that, last night, included an all-night prayer festival at a huge church in Mt Wellington.

And now, right on opening, with money he nicked from his dad—it's where Abe slept last night, and where they were this morning—Kid's got them a family pass to Auckland Zoo.

He bends to check Abraham, who's already straining at the straps of the new stroller their church gave them when they committed to the congregation.

'Up!' says Abraham. 'Get! Up!' The boy's eyes are bulgy and the skin around them is red like the material the stroller's made of.

'He looks thirsty,' says Kid, working on not talking too fast. 'He's thirsty, do you think?'

'How would I know?' goes Vanessa, distracted by the zoo map she's holding.

Her tone threatens Kid's buzz.

'You thirsty, mate?' asks Kid.

'Up!' goes the boy. 'Out!'

'An ice cream?' says Kid. 'See the animals, eh? Then we'll get a Trumpet.'

Nodding seriously—Kid likes his son's serious reaction to treats—the boy goes, 'Yes,' and then sits back a little so Kid can fit one of the straps better over his shoulder.

'We have to watch too much sugar,' says Vanessa.

'That's from Trudy, is it?' goes Kid, and then, as he does when he's pissed with his wife, when he wants her to see how well he knows his son, he devotes himself to entertaining Abraham with a series of animal sounds and faces.

That first Sunday, church assigned them each a mentor. Trudy wouldn't be a lot older than Vanessa, but she has a girl and twin boys and her ex-cop, polished-head husband owns two late-night dairies in Taupo. Mostly, she tells Vanessa how to parent, which is stupid, fucking stupid, because Kid does all the looking after of Shawn . . . Abraham . . . *Sorry, sorry God, sorry my Lord, sorry for the f-word.* Edgar, that's Kid's mentor, says becoming Christian comes down to changing thought patterns. That words stem from thoughts and actions stem from words and Edgar's got a super-long fringe combed back over a bald spot—do all serious Christians wear their hair weirdly?—and he likes to look around at them in church, smiling, as if that'll help what the preacher's saying sink in better, or maybe, and this is what Vanessa thinks, he grins so much because he's got a hard-on for Kid.

Kid who, queuing for the zoo tickets, took 20mg of Ritalin he bought at the festival from a guy who also sold him a can of high-strength beer and a joint laced (apparently) with MDMA, both of which Kid consumed last night without telling Vanessa, but church always talks about being true to yourself, so, though Kid would normally pretend the money he stole was his—that he'd come by it in some cool/mysterious way—he now gives up the animal faces and says, neutralising the drug-lie with a stealing truth, 'I pinched money from Dad, but he would have just spent it on smokes. If he didn't want me taking it, why leave his wallet out?'

But all he gets for his confession from Vanessa is a bored look. 'So, we're going in?'

Bouncing out of his crouch, Kid gets into position behind the stroller, making more revving noises and starting them towards where zoo staff are scanning the information on people's tickets as they enter. 'Where's first?' he goes, trying to keep everything upbeat.

But lately Vanessa won't even answer when he asks something. Won't even look at him, will just sit there gaping at Abe, or her phone or whatever. Like . . . like Kid might as well not even be there. He's used to it, but still it pisses him off, and he speeds up, getting well ahead of her.

African Plains, says a sign with an arrow. *Tiger Country*, says another.

'Tiger Country!' goes Kid, talking forward to Abe and taking aim with the stroller. There's a glass enclosure, but all you see are big-leafed shrubs and areas of thick, deep-green grass and stuff.

'Any tigers?' goes Kid, stopping, getting back down to Abe's level, and showing the boy how to scan the glass.

The boy jerks forward against the straps and Kid does another animal, this time a tiger, with wild eyes and his hands as its claws. 'Tigers, *mate*,' he says, like they're Australians.

The boy smiles, but jerks forward and back again, and Kid gets back behind the stroller. When it comes to Abe, what he's found is that to avoid meltdowns, best approach is to keep everything fast-moving.

Vanessa's at a hip-height concrete fence. Standing there with the crumpled map, looking at her phone.

'Any tigers?' says Kid, pulling in beside her.

This one's more pit than enclosure. Sort of, what's the word? Medieval. Rock walls, pushed-over trees with planks between them, a banked-off area of shallow water, all of it sloping down from a low, prison-looking sort of building, where all the tigers probably are.

It hasn't really come on yet, but Kid feels guilty he's taken a pill and she hasn't, so, and though he knows it's try-hard, he attempts to get something back from Vanessa by saying, 'Wouldn't want to fall in, eh? What was it? Them lions and us Christians?'

Fast, like she was waiting for him to say it, like he's retarded, she says, 'It's tigers in here, not lions,' and even before she then, in a slightly nicer way, says, 'The elephants and whatever are that way,' he's already left her, pedalling his feet fast against the asphalt, swooping in on the *African Plains* sign, the sign that points to a boardwalk, from where, spread beneath them, you see a pale dirt paddock, fences and, once your eyes figure them out, giraffes and zebras.

'And ooh, what's that?' Kid says. Wanting to be the one who does the showing, he gets to the front of the stroller, unclips, hoists Abraham up and points. 'That big bird!'

The boy looks for a moment then says, 'Ice. Cream!' putting his hand into Kid's mouth.

Through the soft bunch of fingers, Kid says, 'Emu.'

'Meerkats are next,' goes Vanessa, coming along the boardwalk.

'Being nice now, are you?'

'Shut up, *Kid*,' she says.

'We're married now, *Vanessa*.'

'So?'

'So?' he parrots.

Abraham goes dead-still when they fight—really taking

it in. It always makes Kid feel guilty, so he joggles his son and smiles, like it's a joke Mum and Dad are having with each other, and then he keeps walking along the boardwalk, towards where other people are standing, all facing the same direction.

According to Vanessa, they're in a hurry. Twice this morning she's said they have to leave no later than 11am in order to drive back, drop the car, walk to their unit where she'll change and then, *fuckin' joy*, get to her shitty sandwich job.

At the meerkat enclosure, it's 9:40am. A short man is made taller by the daughter on his shoulders. An old man sets up a tripod. Christian jokes aside, Kid likes the support church provides. That, and the Sunday routine of getting ready and going. Vanessa's habit, when she's not doing the breakfast shift, is to sit around until the last possible minute, change out of her pyjamas in a hurry, and rush to work. Lazy, bloody lazy—being in pyjamas means she always has an excuse for not taking Abraham outside to play.

Little big-eyed creatures with paws are zipping around trails they've made with their zipping around. Abraham's getting heavy and Kid puts him back in the stroller.

'Meerkats, eh?' he says, making his hand into one of the animals, having it stop and look in front of the boy's face.

More and more, Vanessa gets on his nerves. Is it worse since they stopped all the partying? Who knows? Anyway, church is somewhere to be on Sunday and because church people 'drop in' all the time, embarrassed-at-the-mess-Vanessa actually helps with the tidying—which is both good, but also irritating. Why doesn't she tidy for him? Plus now they don't run out of milk or biscuits . . . Overall, since going to church, Kid's more fed up with Vanessa but his life's easier, and that's made life better for Abraham.

He steers towards the end of the enclosure where signs point to *Elephants*. Kid's body is starting to feel tired. They were up all night after all, but his brain's doing all this sharp thinking and looking at tall Vanessa—up there on her long legs—and wanting to acknowledge the slight improvement in their life with something kind, he goes close, looking at her out of the corner of his eye, and says, 'I want to lie down with you.'

It must have come out louder than he planned, because a meerkat-watching woman wearing shiny exercise pants looks around.

'Got that from the Bible, did you?' says Vanessa, but he's almost got a smile.

'Sex shouldn't be something you just do,' whispers Kid, which was something Edgar said to him, and was now a thing they both liked to say when they were feeling close, when they weren't arguing about who did what around the place in terms of earning money, cleaning the toilet or changing nappies.

Abraham thrusts forward again, and this time, quick as, Kid tips the stroller back, causing Abraham a fast reverse.

'Careful!' says Vanessa.

'I got it,' says Kid.

'You're high,' says Vanessa.

Kid ignores her. 'Let's just carry him. We're going to have to lift him in and out all the way around.'

Sighing—she's always bloody sighing—she looks at him and then at the stroller. 'What about that?'

'I'll run back to the car. Meet you at the elephants.'

'Whatever,' says Vanessa, 'but you're high. I'm telling Edgar.'

Forgetting *kind*, Kid uses his sarcastic, I'm-way-more-intelligent-than-you tone: 'Don't just rush around, you know? Let him look, try to teach him something.'

Vanessa bends at the front of the stroller and gets Abraham. When she stands, her face is red from gravity and the lift. 'I have been to a zoo before, you know.'

Ignoring her again Kid says, in a softer way, 'See you soon, mate,' but when he ducks in to kiss his son Vanessa swivels fast, so all he ends up kissing is the air where his son's cheek had been.

'Hey, fuck,' Kid says, and to make it worse, when he says that, because of the way she's got him, it's only Shawn who sees his angry face, and worse still, as he's trying to smile and make a happy pose for his son, Vanessa swivels again, so he's wide-open and grinning for his tall wife, who takes the opportunity, in victory, to give him the finger.

It burns. Freaky giraffe wife! Right there she's wiped all the good he's done for them this morning.

The 'up' buzz of Ritalin switches to blood pouring to the surface of his skin, to sweat, soaking the undies he wore all day yesterday, and all night, and kept on this morning, and are now slime, while the tighter parts, the waistband, the bands round his thighs, those parts start to itch, and, and . . . Forgiveness, forgiveness is a big word at church. Love, mercy. Christ and God, obviously, but forgiveness comes up a lot.

There they go, disappearing under a sign that says *Watering Hole*. Is Shawn looking? In case he is, Kid's waving, waving one hand and scratching with the other, but the boy doesn't see. They had bed bugs at Waikeria, little fuckers that hook their jaws in, and the itching at what the jaws did brings on these volcano-skin-things that itch even worse, and right now, around his waist and thighs, the itching's way worse than that, so, standing, legs crossed, like he's desperate to piss, there's only one thing left to do.

Run. Sprint the boardwalk with the stroller. And ah, *yes, Jesus*, that feels better. Wind up the legs of his shorts cools sweat, easing the itch. So he runs faster, zigging and zagging, passing people who stare into the stroller as if he'd be stupid enough to do this sort of speed with Shawn aboard.

Looking after Shawn all the time, Kid sometimes feels old and past it. Way past the point where there was still the possibility of being someone, but running with this weight ahead makes him feel strong and young and here, in front of him on the boardwalk, is one of those older families with the pretty mum and neatly bearded dad and two kids with zoo T-shirts—them with their sensible fucking shoes, and organisation—and Kid's high-speed dash has brought on a good destructive feeling, so he aims right into the middle, scattering them like a water-blaster, and, and . . . and what Kid would never admit, to anyone, is the 24/7 terror he feels at losing his son.

He loves Shawn. So much. He doesn't know about

Vanessa. When they drank all the time he experienced what he'd have called love, but maybe that was just a good feeling off the booze, combined with actual post-prison female company, but the thing between him and Shawn, that's pure. Or holy. If holy means clean and sort of unbreakable, like a wide white roll of NASA-strength plastic, rolling on and on . . .

Tight left at the sign for *Savannah*. Still moving, still getting wind up around his grots. Past two staff members still scanning tickets.

Not that love was there right away. Love came in little leaps. Like the time Shawn was, what? Ten months? The snooker was on telly, and somehow coloured balls going this way and that got the wee man laughing and pointing and wanting to climb through the TV onto that big green table. Or when Kid stayed up all night, holding his boy's tiny body as it went stiff and vomited, holding the tiny, hot body as it went as limp, wiping his face and hands and feet with a flannel he kept cool in a big bowl of ice.

'Sacrifice,' Kid now says, remembering another church word.

He's left the itch way back on the boardwalk and now, no doubt, the Ritalin's in. His thoughts are clear and positive, but his brain is stressed from duelling with Vanessa. The other name she uses on him is Jailbird, sometimes sweetly, other times, real mean and . . . Hold on, what's this? There, by the gift shop, three hire-strollers. Why not save his energy and leave their stroller here?

'In camouflage,' Kid says, wiping his face which shines in the shop window from where a huge toy warthog stares.

Vanessa will be amazed he was so fast and, when she sees their stroller here in plain sight, when she sees the simplicity of it, she'll accept he's worth at least something.

'In the meantime . . .' he goes. In the meantime, surprise them at the elephants with elephant-sized ice creams. Be the steady hand Edgar talks about, be that rock.

So, still sweating, Kid takes time making the stroller seem like all the other strollers, making it seem 'ready' for hire, before resetting his cap and sunglasses and swaggering back in the direction of his son and wife, swaggering, because what's building here (forget Edgar's steady-hand shit), what's the obvious outcome of this no-sleep-drug-morning, of this getting wrung out by Vanessa, of getting worked up about life in general, and Shawn specifically, is the urge—the same basic sequence that led Kid to do the thing that put him in prison—to draw attention to himself, probably not by doing a good thing, because getting good attention takes time: making the Warriors, gaining awesome success through music or business.

Waving his ticket like it's a bundle of cash, Kid goes past the ticket scanners again, and here, what's this? Lots of people at the tiger enclosure with more people hurrying and a voice over a speaker announcing, 'Breakfast time in tiger territory,' and what's best right now? Run around getting ice creams and having the stupid things drip all over his hands while trying to find Vanessa who'll be whizzing Shawn past polar bears and monkeys and whatever else—guaranteeing he learns nothing about anything—or falling in behind this excited crowd? Falling into a situation where at least the possibility exists for him to show church, Vanessa and that rich-arse board-walking family precisely—that's *his* word, not God's—precisely the man they expect when they see an ex-con, unemployed druggie, in basketball shorts and a crooked cap.

And so, Kid's running again, this time towards the tigers, where the female, Molek—over a speaker, a zoo-keeper's saying she's the *wildest* of their tigers—is, apparently, about to feed.

'Today's menu includes freshly killed chook, though of course they prefer live prey,' goes the keeper.

Kid stops at the crowd's fringe and, with the overly polite voice he learnt in prison—*excuse me sir, ma'am, excuse me*—he works his way to the concrete wall. Beneath him there's two metres to the narrow walkway that circles six or seven metres above the enclosure.

'Fully extended,' goes the zoo-keeper, 'an adult tiger's claws are thirteen centimetres long, while their canines are longer than your middle finger.'

In his jungle-green uniform, safari hat and mirror sunglasses, he's further around the walkway, holding a sack which, from its shape, looks like it contains more of the feathery, crooked-legged carcasses that match the one he has by the head and is dangling well above the tiger—Molek—who's stood there, sipping with her nostrils—and yeah, bro—actually licking her lips.

What if Shawn fell? You see it on the news and shit—a young fella ends up getting half-eaten and batted around an enclosure. Then someone jumps in. The parent—he/she jumps in to distract the gorilla, or lion, or tiger. Being that person would be something major in a man's life. Dropping down, turning your body into a shield for the child.

Kid tips forward off his feet so he's half over the railing and looks. From this position, he'd forward roll down onto the walkway, and then . . . There, jump from the walkway onto that springy grass—you'd have to go hard to clear that knifey-looking tree branch, hitting that would cost skin, and what else you'd be risking, at the least, would be leg injuries: a dislocated knee, a broken ankle, but any of that would be minor compared to what would be next—facing off against old Molek . . .

'Excuse me? Hey!'

It's the zoo-keeper, aiming the chicken like it's a gun. 'Back from there, please.'

Kid looks at Molek, who looks at the chicken's changed position, and then at the zoo-keeper who's smiling, but in a serious way. Kid tips back, comes away from the wall, turns. People that before were right up close have moved back. Now there's a half-moon of bare concrete—like a stage—and isn't this better than damp washing hanging from every imaginable part of their unit, melting ice creams wrecking the borrowed car's upholstery, and arguing with Vanessa all the way home to Hamilton?

Maybe it's the quiet—all the people are staring like he's one of the animals—or the way Kid's holding his upper half because, still sounding worried, the zoo-keeper says, 'Sir?'

It's hot. Suddenly very hot, and when Kid strips off his hoodie his bat's wings flip free and fly him up, so now where he's standing is the narrow ridge of that high wall, facing his crowd, and if it's good enough for the preacher at church to go around palms pointed at heaven, then it's good enough for Kid.

'Sir?' he hears again.

'My God!' he hears.

To savour this—*now* he's someone—to slow it down, Kid turns carefully back to the enclosure, arms still wide, like instead of a jump it's a dive at the Olympics he's going to make. While below, made smaller by his increased height, Molek edges in his direction as the zoo-keeper—he's laid down the chicken—speaks in a hard voice into a walkie-talkie.

See? Easy as. Kid matters. People are talking, people are worried—look at Crocodile Dundee there all stiff-necked and scared. Soon the whole country will hear—today at Auckland Zoo a young man jumped—nah, leaped—into a tiger enclosure. Leaped *onto* a tiger—because how it looks is that Kid will land on Molek. She's come across and now she backs up and waits, sitting on that springy grass, her head and narrowed eyes and wet, just-open mouth, all of it satellite-dishing up at him. How will church explain this one away? What will Trudy say? Or her bald-arsed husband? You could own all the supermarkets in Taupo, and the biggest fucking car—

'But none of that counts for shit when you're one on one with a tiger,' goes Kid, setting his feet wide, and though he's primed for this, and therefore calm, he starts crying—for Shawn, of course—which is just the sort of weak-arsed shit that's always caused Kid to finally do whatever it is he's threatening, and so, keeping his arms out for balance, he squats, fills his wings, and—

'Kid?'

Vanessa. Straightaway he's angry. How fast must she have rushed Shawn through all the other enclosures to be here now? But the anger doesn't last, because the other sound, the one he now realises has been sirening closer and closer, the sound cutting through the Ritalin and his need to be more than just the idiot charged with rescuing Shawn's plastic planes from the toilet's S-bend, is Shawn crying.

His son, behind him, crying. The crying he does when he's really worked up about something (like that time a car alarmed right outside their unit) or badly hurt, or only a little bit hurt but massively overtired. Hiccupping and hyperventilating while also screaming. Kid starts to turn, but then stops and stays, facing Molek. Isn't it better for the boy to know that his dad did something? That he *acted.* At least once. That isn't suicide, it's—what do you call it? Martyrdom. What Shawn would always have, what no one, not Trudy, not Edgar, would be able to take away, would be the day Dad rodeoed on a real live tiger.

That's way better than just being this spineless bum-tool who stands around getting steamrollered by the world every couple of days.

Isn't it?

Kid looks at Molek who twitches her tail, and stays there watching.

Like she's answering his question with her own question, Vanessa again goes, 'Kid?'

A tiger's down there waiting for lunch, so she's scared, but is there also *need* in her voice? Wanting to check and desperate to see his boy, Kid, way less confidently—his legs are starting to spaghetti—goes back around. And there, there they are, and right away its obvious what's wrong.

Poos. A bad one. Sometimes—no matter how good you have the nappy attached—these nuclear bombs go off that blow shit from feet to neck. It's on Vanessa's T-shirt, it's dripping out from under Shawn's shorts, dripping off his shoes as he joggles miserably in Vanessa's arms, tugging at her face and hair. Vanessa who looks hot and scared. Running around trying to find Kid she's got all stressed and Shawn's picked up on her suffering so now he's hot from the heat, hot from the crying, and hard-out burning up from the shame of all the people who, no doubt, have been staring at Vanessa like she's some sort of dumb-arse.

'*Kid*,' goes Vanessa again, who, yeah, as well as scared looks angry.

Wipes and nappies are back in the stroller. And aren't there also clean shorts and an empty Pak'n'Save bag for dirty clothes?

The choice is martyrdom or just getting down, running for the stroller and finding a cool, quiet place to change Shawn, while Vanessa uses her nice singing voice as a distraction. At home Kid can put the shorts in that red bucket he bought last week for soaking.

That stuff—nappies, wipes, clean and dirty washing—banks up behind Kid, almost pushing him down off the wall. But then, among the crowd, sort of flooding out Shawn and Vanessa, are three ZOO SECURITY uniforms. Motherfuckers about to tell him what to do, about to muscle him off the wall and take him wherever . . .

Shawn can't see that. But Kid can't leave Shawn.

'Sir,' goes one man.

Which is when Kid remembers what Edgar once said about options: how there's one choice, the other choice, and Jesus.

'Sir?'

Re-engage those wings and fly the fuck out of here. That'll be something Shawn will never forget. And so that's what Kid does. Stands tall on his legs that are strong again, smiles at Shawn and Vanessa, opens his wings—the sound is of giant coins clicking into two giant slots—and rises . . .

The Swimmers

Eric held the door and Russell went through. Eric followed. They both had sports bags. There were damp patches by the long wooden benches where other men had stood after swimming, but the changing room was empty.

'Here we go,' said Eric.

'Yep,' said Russell.

There was a faint echo. Cold came up off the concrete.

As always, they put their bags on the same area of benching. Some hooks around the tiled walls held jackets and pants, but most played it safe, carrying their belongings poolside, leaving them in the cubby holes there.

Eric and Russell swam every Tuesday. They had for twenty-five years. At the end of each swim, they raced. Freestyle, one hundred metres. Eric had never lost, though what he'd kept from Russell was that over that long period he'd taken swimming lessons, trained with weights and done lots of extra swimming to make sure he kept hold of his winning streak. Eric's other big secret was that something had once happened with him and Russell's wife, Alice.

'Morning!'

It was the one-legged cleaner. A pool-issue polo, shorts, his metal above-the-knee leg.

'Morning,' said Eric, in his clipped ex-principal's voice.

Hands worrying his bag's zip, Russell stayed quiet.

Eric always urinated before his swim so he followed the cleaner out of the changing rooms and into the shower/toilet area. With all the winning he did, this was his domain. In other domains Russell might have been in charge—after all, before his retirement, he'd been high up at the university, but here, in the pool, the changing rooms, the showers, even out in the car park, Eric felt in charge.

At the urinal he unslung and, after a moment or two, it started.

Alice—her face round and shiny as a cherry—was dead now. So too Una. And the kids were long gone. Russell's three in places like Hong Kong; Eric's in Christchurch and Auckland. Russell had a small unit at Summerset; Eric still lived in the family home. They both drove. They both had other interests. Didn't Russell attend a French-speaking class? Or was it cooking?

Eric joggled and waited. Joggled again and waited. No rush. Russell took ages getting changed, rotating, arms out, around his sports bag like some police robot dealing with a suspicious package. Eric bounced at his knees to get the last drips and then zipped.

'Okay,' he said.

No way would he admit it, but week to week this was his highlight. This was him most alive. Beating Russell—he never tired of it.

'Guess who's got new togs?' he said, walking back to where naked Russell was stapled over, bringing his yellow shorts over his feet. Staying bent, Russell worked the shorts past his knees and up around his waist. Last week he'd brought the wrong bag down from the cubby holes, getting as far as putting on the other man's trousers before realising. 'I don't think these are my clothes,' he'd said, taking what looked like a calculator from a pocket.

Eric had laughed so much he worried he might break a rib.

Wouldn't happen to him. He knew his clothes and kept them clean and up to date. Track suits or, as today, jeans, an open-neck shirt and a colourful jersey—the jam-coloured one he now brought up over his head and folded neatly beside his bag.

The memo finally received, Russell said, 'New togs, eh?'

Concerning, actually, collecting the wrong clothes. Who would Eric race if Russell lost his marbles? Without winning, swimming wouldn't be fun. Taking off his shirt, he folded it beside his jersey. Una, she'd always liked the pride he had in his appearance. It wasn't so common back then. Men nowadays with their tattoos and hair gel! Too much by half—tidy with a hint of style was as far as you needed to go. Taking out his towel and new togs—red drawstring, designs like lightning bolts in a wide-framed strip down the thigh—Eric filed the folded clothes into his bag.

Una, ah Una, the times they had together!

'The good times, the *good* times,' Eric found himself saying as he pulled on his new togs.

Already Russell wore his goggles high on his forehead. 'Right?' he said, getting a hold of his bag.

Eric gathered his gear and they went out of the changing rooms and past the showers where one-leg was using a hose.

'Good swimming, gentlemen,' he said.

Smiling at the cleaner, getting ready for the handrail, Russell switched his sports bag from one hand to the other. Ahead, Eric started on the stairs. The colourful waistband of the togs biting into wrinkled, hairless skin. The bluish kidney-level mole. Eric.

Taking the handrail, Russell started. One foot onto a step, the other onto the same step. Back to that first foot. The sound of the pool—school kids, aqua-aerobics music. Wet, ribbed tiles under his feet. Thinking about boarding planes. Up steep stairs from the tarmac. Momona's cold wind. Him and Alice off on some trip. With the kids, without them, some work-related junket. Looking up Russell found Eric gone—always so keen to get a lane! Eric, laughing so much about that clothes mix-up he'd ended in a crouch.

'Ended the colour of beetroot,' said Russell.

He never thought about Eric. Especially not since that Northland trip they all took. But even before that. Vanilla's a way you might describe him. His conversations. About driving Dunedin—all the traffic, all the road works. And pizza toppings that froze well and reheated best. But swimming with him was a habit and Russell liked those. Thursdays he discussed movies with George. Sundays he cooked for Edward and Tina. Tuesdays he swam. And what wasn't to enjoy about the racing? It was good to feel his heart hammer. He never won, but so what? You had to be realistic, you had to be rational. Eric had better technique. He was fitter—clearly, he swam other days. Also, it amused Russell how serious Eric got—huffing and puffing and scowling around at the water before they took off. *Ready, go!* like the Olympics.

Being underwater was good, the way sound came in with the oxygen when you breathed, the feeling of really needing breath, not taking it so much for granted. Had Alice once said something like that? How it brought your lungs to the fore. Alice. A permanent ponytail. Short and shiny with the light of the world in her eyes. Like a figure atop one of those old sports trophies.

Emerging into the cathedral—high-ceilinged, huge clocks, Rod Stewart for the aerobics ladies, the Danyon Loader mural—Russell headed towards where Eric was carefully settling his bag in a cubby hole, getting it just so, as if someone from a decor magazine was poised to photograph his folded clothes.

Eric surveyed the pool. Aerobics, school kids getting lessons in the far lanes. A disabled man with a helper ploughing up and down the near lane. And, unusually, the middle lanes busy with swimmers. In the far end of the pool—it was divided by a central wall—people in miniature kayaks practised Eskimo rolls. Eric made big circles with his arms. Here came Russell, watching each step as though it was ice he was on. What about the diving pool? It was twenty-five metres long and three lanes were kept for swimming—Slow by the side of the pool, Medium, Fast. The rest left for the aqua-joggers to make their circuits. Darker with the depth, and warmer than the main pool, Eric swam there sometimes when he was by himself, but he preferred to race in the main pool.

Russell, *finally.*

'The diving pool?' asked Eric, switching to a triceps stretch.

Russell nodded, going to the cubby holes with his gear.

Leaning on a pillar, Eric attended to his quadriceps. Didn't the togs feel good! Firm as rubber bands around his thighs and rump. He couldn't wait to get in, couldn't wait to race. Rearing up out of the water, making strong beautiful shapes with his arms, his legs the propeller powering him along. Russell bobbing there in his wake, Russell there like laundry—hard racing didn't involve friendship, during hard racing competitors were your enemies, they were your victims.

'And for Christ's sake, Russell, remember where you put your bag,' said Eric in a hard loud voice, and to emphasise his words he slapped his chest, bringing out a faint mark that had faded by the time he stormed to the head of the Medium lane and dived out over the deep water, glorying in the pre-penetration moment.

Eric had bossed him before, but this chest slapping stuff was new. Was Russell a child at one of the primary schools Eric used to rule? Included with the new togs were there instructions on being an arsehole? Packing his bag away he examined his humiliation. A slick sensation out his armpits over his skin. His dry tongue pressed hard against his teeth. No, he wouldn't take it.

Turning, he prepared to use some language against Eric but too late, the prick was flying out over the pool, grinning as his hands arrowed the water.

A froggy sound came up out of Russell's throat. He tried to camouflage it with a cough, because a woman in togs—tattooed arms, a sympathetic look—carrying a toddler was there.

The mum looked ready to speak. She'd obviously heard, but what would she say?

How dare he talk like that to you.

Or, directing outrage at Russell: *Why would you let him talk like that?*

Eric's tone was way worse than what he'd said, and what he'd said was bad enough.

Russell made a broad smile for the woman, who swallowed whatever was on her mind and moved off. And so, finally, he got himself going towards the pool, to where, from the side of the pool, the ladder went into the Slow lane. Turning, finding the first rung, his hands around the uprights, the water around his feet, now shins, now knees, now flooding his groin. Getting old ate shit. That's what Alice said. Not being able to get things to work. Medical situations. Leakages. But activities and social interactions you'd chosen weren't supposed to include humiliation.

Russell took a breath, went under, found the back wall with the balls of his feet and kicked off. Bubbles streamed from his nose as he surfaced and made two strokes. Then he breathed, bringing his arm over, kicking, feeling better in the water than usual, feeling his anger at Eric translate to extra strength, giving him the idea that maybe he was up for today's race, giving him the idea that today's race might present an opportunity for a little revenge.

And, as he tilted his face at the ceiling's great struts and filled his lungs, nearing the end of the first of his twelve warm-up lengths, his thoughts flew back twenty-five years. To that week in Northland. Because if rage at Eric was the fuel his swimming needed, was there another time to consider?

The talk had been of an overseas trip, but in the end the women picked Kerikeri. Vineyards, beaches, waterfalls. There was a chocolate factory, tennis courts, the possibility of trips to Cape Reinga, the Mangonui fish and chip shop and Waitangi. Or maybe, as Una put it, they would just sit around drinking gin and tonic.

She'd just got the green light after a cancer scare. Russell and Alice's youngest was finally on his OE. Health and freedom, that's what they were celebrating. And they were doing it in style. Una had booked them into a sprawling restored villa set on a hill surrounded by paddocks where silver horses grazed, grapes grew and pheasants flared, backgrounded by the most beautiful sunsets Russell had seen.

Smiling Americans owned the place. They greeted the two couples, gave them iced flutes of champagne, carried off their luggage, and then came back to take breakfast orders and show them their rooms. Russell and Alice were in the main house. A king-size bed. A marble, two-person, walk-in shower. From their private deck a view over a grand lawn, kōwhai bubbling with tūī, and a narrow opening between two huge rhododendrons to a path that led through a citrus orchard to Eric and Una's fully appointed cottage with its large outdoor bathtub you heated by lighting a fire underneath.

At that stage, Russell and Eric had been swimming for five years. After dinner on Tuesdays. They talked more then. Mostly Eric. Policies he'd put in place at whatever school he was head of. Teachers he'd hired and fired. Weekends the women would sometimes bring them together for drinks or dinner. Una and Alice had nursed at Queen Mary in the late Fifties and stayed in touch since. It was them who'd suggested the men—neither of whom was exactly festooned with friends—do their little swimming thing together.

Russell worked hard back then. Lecturing, publishing papers, overseeing a gaggle of PhD students. Quietly ambitious. Quietly stubborn. 'Quietly a bit of an arsehole,' Alice had once said to him.

Anyway, he'd have preferred not to holiday with Eric and Una. Eric was a blowhard. Eric with his leather jackets, thin ties and bad taste in food. Eric shifting in his seat to take in Alice's arse. Una was okay. Funny when she'd had a couple of drinks and started needling Eric. But Alice was the only person Russell ever wanted to holiday with.

No way, though, was she having any of Russell's just-the-two-of-them stuff. 'I'm not spending my holiday listening to endless talk about your precious department.'

Marvellous Alice, mother-of-the-twentieth-century Alice. Her vodka on ice, her political views. Marching down George Street, marching on the Octagon. No

Nukes. No Tour. Alice wearing that underwear she'd buy through a catalogue one of the boys found once. Dead now, and Russell had never recovered. He'd never been the same. Just to cook for her one more time, to hear her voice break at the beauty of a plate he'd set for her. 'Oh, Russell? Oh, golly fucking gosh!'

Golly gosh. Russell stopped after his sixth length and took off his goggles. Up the vacant Fast lane's rope two joggers chatted. Sun cut through the tall windows looking over the car park, its glare making the end of the pool all but disappear. And here, out of that sun, came Eric. The big dome of his head, the strong arms windmilling, hitting the wall, eyeballing Russell, turning, plunging under, surfacing, churning back up the lane.

A few years after Northland, Una's cancer came back and she died. They'd stopped seeing them as a couple, but Alice had kept up with Una and she'd grieved. But death didn't touch Russell. His kids he cared for. And Alice. But really, no one else. A cold streak then, and within a cold streak there's usually a cruel streak. Everyone has negative traits, though. Being some wrinkly widower doesn't change that.

Russell farting about as usual. Stopping every length. It annoyed Eric to think other people might mistake him for his training partner. Slumped over the lane rope as though he'd had a stroke. Emphasising his energy, Eric hit the wall and turned, sank deep, bent his knees and blasted off, surfacing but not breathing for three, four, five hard strokes. These two ducks for example, jogging up the outer lane rope, what would they think? Head down, he powered past, taking in the rotations of their lovely thick legs.

Tall, bony Una. Her clavicles. The edges of her shoulder blades, knee bones like little turtle shells, long pianist's fingers. The care she took of her fingernails. Playing the piano in the spare room when he got home from work. In there with the heavy red wine she drank. Getting angry at him that time at the hospice for never having done her the respect of entering and listening. 'What if I'd been playing naked? You'd have bloody well gone for that!'

Her suddenly laughing at that. Him laughing too, her dying and him not even able to explain he was shy to be so moved. That, and having no words to describe the beauty of her music . . .

Eric was a doer. A leader. He talked with great sweeps of his long arms. He used volume to impose his will. He was, by the time he retired, Dunedin's most respected principal. He'd got awards from the mayor; he'd had an annex at Grant's Braes School named after him. Direct, strong, a missile from a U-boat, swift S's with his hands, roiling the water behind him, smashing into the end wall, glancing at the pool's timer—it told no lies, he was *on* today—plunging back, eating up another length.

Surprisingly, it was Una who'd made all the big decisions. Houses to buy, cars to buy, renovations, holidays. Eric was impatient. No one ever asked—and no one ever would—but if they did, he wouldn't be too proud these days to say he dreamed about her every night. Playing her piano, nailing him with her sharp tongue, cuddled up beside him, her morning Milo, the way she cut her toast.

He'd been a good husband. To her, he'd mattered.

Ahead, Russell was gesturing at him to stop.

Alice that time in the outdoor bath. Russell's Alice. Not that he, Eric, had been a saint.

He stopped. 'What?'

'Why don't we start racing?'

Eric cleared snot. The sun had gone and everything had dimmed. He turned. Here were the aqua-joggers. Glasses, bobbed grey hair. He drew his hand down his face. 'Morning!'

The women nodded. The one in lipstick showed her teeth. Eric's deltoids and pecs throbbed. Given the choice he'd be in a school hall somewhere, in just these togs, in front of a crowd of women, rotating slowly on some raised podium. Winning their admiration. Well, why not? Nothing wrong with his bloody libido! Nothing wrong with admitting he missed the way Una used to appreciate the shape he kept his body in.

'Racing?' he went in a loud voice.

'I feel good today. Let's have two races. A sprint, plus a longer one.'

Eric exaggerated surprise. 'Overdo the Metamucil this morning, Russell?'

Russell stood on the low wall at the head of his lane. Rod Stewart had stopped. On the pool's corner, with its view over this pool and the main one, two lifeguards were swapping posts. Cornering in slow motion, the aqua-joggers watched as Russell bent, making his arms loose as tentacles, creeping his toes to the edge of the wall.

'We're having a diving start?' said Eric, sounding genuinely surprised.

Russell couldn't stay down long—his hamstrings drawn too tight, some of his internal organs pinched. 'Might as well,' he grunted.

'Ian Thorpe, eh?' said Eric in a voice loud enough for the joggers and even lifeguards to hear. But now he got himself into a crouch.

Russell glanced at Eric's feet—wrinkled skin, a pachyderm's toenails. Not that Russell could talk. Not that this was the time to be comparing feet.

'Ready?' he asked. Right away, he dived, 'Go!' he shouted, sailing over the water.

'*Bastard*,' he heard as he hit.

Wanting to give the impression of determined racing, he pulled hard for a few strokes, but Eric must have made a good long shallow dive, because he was level already. Then he was past, stirring the water in Russell's lane, making it harder to get good purchase, not that that mattered to Russell, because, wanting to conserve energy, he'd already slowed right down.

Eric hit the wall and came up fast, badly needing air. Proper sprinting was anaerobic so he'd done the twenty-five without breath. Clinging to the pool edge he pulled off his goggles. Light spots pocked his vision, the sensation of something milking acid came from his gut. He blinked at the calm water between his chest and the wall. Chlorine. Pinching on his upper nose where the plastic joining the eye parts of his goggles bit. Water dripped from his armpit hair. His breathing didn't ease—came instead in heaves, like throwing up in reverse. A car accident. Cancer on the cancer ward. Here even, being fished out for a bit of CPR. As long as it didn't happen at home, on the kitchen floor while his Sunday night toastie pie cooked. Smelling that, while dying under the ceiling Una painted every couple of years. Not having a face, any face, there as you died. That's what had scared Una. Now it was what scared him.

But suddenly the tension in his diaphragm eased—that sprint must have created a major oxygen imbalance—and his vision cleared. Coming back to himself he turned. Russell trying to get him at the start like that! Russell coming on, slower than a bloody dugong. No one was dying. Not today. Dying of boredom, maybe. Because, here, finally, Russell touched, turned, and lifted up his goggles.

'Fast today, Eric,' he said. 'Must be those togs.'

Vulnerable, still feeling a little fear, Eric said, 'You're looking okay out there.'

Russell didn't seem to hear. Already he had his goggles down. 'Let's do a two-hundred—gives you no excuse not to lap me. Ready?'

And before Eric could suggest a delay, before he could try to engage Russell in conversation to extend that delay, before he could even get his goggles on, Russell said 'Go!' and kicked off the wall.

The joggers were watching. There was nothing else to do. Putting his goggles on, he took a breath, sank and kicked off.

*

Russell settled into his stroke. The grid of square blue tiles and, when he breathed, the diving boards' different levels. Water's sound in his ears. The ragged breathing back there. Eric's red head a siren. Was tricking him into this urgent racing state dangerous? Other than its age, was there anything wrong with Eric's heart? Russell didn't know. His sole goal was inflicting a little psychological pain. He had controlled people in the past—playing one department head off against another, other times bringing certain key players in close to guarantee funding. Times were, on an evening walk, Russell would be elaborating on some work situation and Alice would stop and just look at him, the tips of her fingers light on her hips.

'What?'

'You don't see?'

'A bit manipulative?'

'A *bit*?'

Now Russell sensed shape beside him and after two more strokes here was Eric. Level already as they closed on the first length. See, nothing wrong with him. What damage could Russell do? An old bastard like him. Eric had juice, and juice was inarguable. Who knew how many lengths he did through the week! Probably he'll lap me easily, Russell thought, watching as Eric hit the wall, turned and came at him. 'Indecent,' Alice had said, 'a man your age with a physique like that. What is it you eat for breakfast, Eric?'

It was the last day of their week away, the four of them lunching at a local winery. Champagne to start, then from white to red. By Alice's breakfast question Eric was having whisky in his coffee, sitting there in short shorts and a short-peaked cycling cap Russell remembers being unreasonably envious of.

And with a real sharky look about him, Eric said: '*Viagra*, Alice.'

Twenty years. Still Russell remembers them all, pre-lunch, watching waterfowl zigging and zagging on a man-made lake. The texture of his whole barely cooked snapper, the delicious mango and chilli salsa the fish came with. Figs and honey they'd shared as a starter.

'Viagra? Una, did he say Viagra?' Alice was drunk. They all were. Celebrating, genuinely, a great week. Walking to a waterfall every morning pre-breakfast. Swimming there and swimming later at different beaches. Sandy, salty, Russell and Alice would shower together and then while Alice snoozed Russell would walk to the township for food to barbecue.

Una made friends with the hosts and two afternoons running they'd lounged on the lawn sharing icy jugs of vodka and tonic. Una who, eyeballing Eric, had said, 'Speak up, Eric. Tell the other children what you said.'

Russell didn't have many other memories of Eric on the holiday: the cycling cap; the time, standing by Russell's barbecue, he reached in, unbidden, and turned a lamb cutlet. Probably what that meant was Russell and Eric had fitted together okay. That Eric hadn't got as far up Russell's nose as expected.

Eric, who now swam towards Russell. Arms stirring, legs hung there kicking. Once he'd passed, Russell kicked a little harder and tried to get his own arms over at a better rate, dragging at the good water, pressing along.

'Doesn't Una know how to rip the balls off *her* man.' Returning from the lunch, he and Alice had adjourned to the cool quiet of their room. Fresh fruit, folded towels, a line-up of boutique teas. Alice stood afoot the freshly turned bed Russell lay on and from their positions in that tableau Alice made her castration comment. Russell, of course, laughed. Though he'd always seen himself as straight down the middle, he loved his wife's crudity.

But then things soured. Alice's approach to an argument was to dip Russell in her sharp good humour and then come up, teeth gnashing. Relaxed, Russell had been drunk and amused by what Eric had said. So, laughing with Alice, he was already letting his mind slide towards what could go on the grill for their final meal when his wife tipped forward on the bed frame and started in. At least Eric paid some attention. At least Eric talked.

'We're holidaying *together*, but you think more about steak than me. Next time you want to go away, why not put one of your precious pieces of porterhouse in a frock and take it to Noosa? I'll stay home, dusting your little degrees.'

Then the attack expanded. Did Russell realise how he'd devalued their relationship?

'Working, working, working. You're barely with me when we're together. Guaranteed, you don't think of me when we're apart. I'm not some goddamn trophy you won and can now forget. Ever heard of a loving gesture? Breakfast, bed? Flowers? Look out the window—they're the colourful things with the bees going in and out.'

*

Eric started his fourth. The rest of this length, then four more. The nausea was gone. Maybe he felt a little sluggish, but, hey, no surprise—look at the mess he'd made of Russell in the sprint! Russell who, quarter of the way through his third length, wasn't actually looking so bad. Eric closed, watching forward before he breathed. Yep, higher in the water, kicking with intent, making good shape with his arms. Had he been practising? It didn't matter—he could look like Dawn Fraser and Eric would still lap him.

But credit was due. A sprint and now a longer race. Maybe that clothes thing had got Russell wanting to blow out some cobwebs. That was Eric's approach. Difficulty getting out of his La-Z-Boy one evening meant the next morning you'd find him doing squats while watching the news on morning telly. Ageing was something to war against. Same with Russell. Putting up a fight today, eh? We'll see about that!

Heading to the wall, Eric moved serious water. The chest tightness coming on, that would be the extra strain on his pecs. If he was burning a little, imagine how Russell must be suffering!

Turning, sinking, Eric kicked into that fifth length. Mind games—getting the most from yourself. He always deployed them. Training alone, he'd imagine Russell was in the next lane, actually competing, while Alice stood poolside, watching them work out, watching Eric annihilate her husband.

Alice. Jesus, just the thought of her was motivating. A

perfect woman. He'd said it to her that last full day of their holiday, Una and Russell floundering around beneath the waterfall, Alice drying her legs with these long strokes. He lost himself around her. His throat ached. In Kerikeri he woke up hard against the mattress, his muck making little speech-bubbles on the bone-coloured sheets Una had thought so much of. Anyway, standing tall, the towel behind her neck—holy moly, her *arms*—Alice had looked square in his eyes and laughed. Pleasantly, but also in a way that stopped Eric saying more.

Breaching, he breathed, thrashed his arm over, hauled it back, rotated, whumped up white water with his kick, and thrashed his opposite arm over. Laugh at this, Alice!

But, hold on, what? Russell, coming already? Eric had eaten way less of his lead than expected. Closing on each other . . . was this right? They'd meet only a bit further down Eric's lane than last time? Was Russell matching him? Level now, they breathed in unison, and there he was. Russell. Cold, stern, unfamiliar as an emperor.

This was racing. Really, in comparison, all Russell had ever done was extend his warm-up. But now he understood. Tempo, it came down to sustaining tempo. Could he keep it another five—make that four—lengths?

Sure as shit. That's what she used to say. Sure as shit, he could do it!

Hitting, not bothering to breathe on the turn, he kicked hard, coming up with a hurricane in his sails.

*

Three lengths for Eric. He whipped his arms over, kicking out a heavy rhythm, the breath on every stroke a gasp. Buck Shelford losing his nut in Nantes. Fitzy, in Jo'burg, holding off the Springboks for the series. Una's dad had been a rugby man—and well, why not? Yes, as an educator Eric couldn't condone the thuggery, but nor would he ever disregard the heroes, the bravery, Meads with his arm that time. When things got hard, men stepped up. They held.

And here came Russell. Splashing as though a crocodile had him, the noise when he breathed a lion's roar. Firing someone—*letting them go*—Eric always experienced this internal lurch just before they entered his office. If it was a matter of over-staffing, maybe he could back down and shuffle some hours to keep them on. With performance-related failure could he cut some slack, could he offer a second or third chance?

Passing Russell, he'd felt it—doubt, doubt he'd always interpreted as fear. Back then his response was anger. Why, in *his* universe, was he experiencing fear? And Russell's determination, his wild animal act, had that same effect now. Fear into anger into resolve. So now, bearing down on the end of his sixth, with it in mind not to back down, to give everything in order to lap Russell, Eric decided on a tumble turn. He'd been practising—often they came off like silk—and when they worked, they took seconds off his times. And so, after one last big stroke, he raised his head, rolled on the vertical, found the wall and, rotating around the horizontal, powered back into battle.

*

Lisbon—the little European tour Russell and Alice took once they'd agreed the kids were old enough to cope with long-haul flights and unpredictable food. Lisbon—its dry heat, aquarium, and bica. Little cups of invigoration, Alice called them. Waking early, jet-lagged, she'd buy them from a vendor near the hotel, returning with two tiny, super-charged coffees—the perfect prelude to holiday love-making. Closing on the wall—three more after this one, but really it was only the next that mattered—Russell could taste it, the coffee on Alice's breath, her tongue heat, the dirty, delicious taste as they kissed.

But, pushing off, that wasn't where his focus was supposed to be. The largest aquarium in Europe. White-bellied manta rays, their undulating wings, flowing smoothly over the dome he and Alice, hips touching, stood beneath. Dawn, the kids asleep in the adjoining room, the slow rotation of a ceiling fan, her perched over his hips, sitting back inch by inch. Or was all that an earlier, even sweatier, holiday in Apia?

Not that Russell believed that in trying to hold off Eric he resembled the beautiful menace of those creatures. The thing in common, the only thing, was that they both moved through water. Acknowledging that, allowing for the wayward arrowing of his brain—Alice, foreign capitals, sex, sex, sex—Russell suddenly felt wrong. His arms didn't want to work. His legs failed, hanging like noodles. On his next stroke, something parted in his shoulder and his arm went so askew he did no more than knock his goggles up his face.

In April, his heart and lungs were eighty years old. His

left hand was eighty too. Raising his head, he watched it wobble into the lane rope. A stroke? Could he even go straight? Was he racing any more?

Other than his bleeding nose, Eric was dynamite. And someone had just lit the fuse, because Russell was *gone*, winging around near the lane rope. Hitting the wall, bonking. That's what they call it, Russell. Mate, you want to look at your nutrition. Feeling blood string from his nose, wanting to amplify the magnitude of his victory, Eric dug harder. Chumming up the dive pool—good nothing hungry is lurking in the depths!

Lapping Russell was a formality. And as usual at this time on a Tuesday, with another crushing victory confirmed, Eric allowed himself to admit he liked, admired, even envied Russell. His status job at the university, his elegant home, the easy way he related to his children, his wife. *His wife.*

Eric breathed towards the side of the pool. The one-legged man was watching. Liking the attention, Eric tried to raise his stroke rate. Deep below, the dark lines of the pool trailed away. Russell and Alice. Always so tight, always so intelligent. Alice that time, turning up at the outdoor bath while Una slept. Split wood smouldering beneath the tub. Stars, but no moon. A night bird calling nearby. Eric naked but for a cold Steinlager.

'Nice night for it,' he had said.

Just above her right knee was a bruise. A new one. Obvious to the man who'd spent the whole holiday mapping the different curves of her legs.

She hadn't answered him—she often didn't. Had just stood, swaying a little, as if down in the vineyards a band played.

Next time Eric breathed pool-side, one-leg had been joined by a lifeguard. Must be they were aware of the racing. Ahead was Russell, beyond was the wall, and with a crowd hadn't Eric better pull another tumble turn? The last one had been so smooth—with people watching an athlete was obliged to entertain.

Bringing his right arm through, getting great traction, he breathed this time towards the diving boards. In the Fast lane, in goggles and a white swim cap, a woman. Breast-stroking up and, as though going downstream, cruising past. The powerful spasm of her frog-kick. Her tense little feet . . .

Perhaps his physiology *was* failing a little. Not surprising given the intensity of the racing. The sensation in his torso . . . with the speed of his swimming was something about to fly apart? That bit in the disaster movie, just before the crash, when the rivets holding the plane's wings start to come loose. Not that it would be his ticker. Or lungs. They were organs he'd cherished—exercise, nutrition, anti-smoking long before anyone else. Probably it was a cold. Though over his career he'd taken no more than a couple of sick days. What did he hear Una say to their eldest that time? 'Your dad's harder to kill than Rasputin.'

Married so long and still Eric couldn't differentiate a compliment from a slight.

Passing Russell now, who was what? Dog-paddling? These people—more were watching, that chick in the Fast lane—would they believe Eric was eighty-three? Not after this tumble turn! And here he raised his head, drew breath and plunged deep, rolling, blindly trying to find the wall with the soles of his feet.

Russell had given his best, but no way was he holding Eric. Having quit the freestyle his body had come back into itself a little. His hard breath still rippled the water by his chin, and his legs weren't really working, but his arms were sort of okay. So, with the help of the rope—he had it like a banister, as though the lane was steep stairs he was going down—he hauled himself along. Towards the far end of the pool, away from the people back there, talking about Eric bleeding into the pool.

First of all, Russell felt implicated, but having checked his vents he could confirm it wasn't him. Not that they'd asked. Paralysed, hyperventilating—must be they saw some real hopeless cases using the Slow lane. Anyway, all down Eric's lane bloody strings of snot hung—witches in the rafters shaking out their hair.

Russell had lost his goggles too. Still moving he groped for them with his left hand. Though would they be needed again? Had he broken Tuesday swimming? Had he broken himself? The feeling in his body was of a fuse shorting. And where was Eric? Not out ahead. Russell looked back—no—and then down. There, wriggling about in the depths. The man from bloody Atlantis! So what if he'd been an arsehole about the clothes and stuff? So what if he'd desired her. Who'd blame him?

Had Eric ever hit Alice? Russell had. Punched her in

that nice room in Kerikeri. A dead leg—that's the way they talked about it much later—when he'd salvaged things, as if the playground term made it better.

From that wisecrack about bees going in and out of flowers, she'd shifted to: 'You'd better watch Eric. He kissed me this morning.'

'What?'

'By the waterfall. The principal's a real Casanova.'

'Bullshit. *Bullshit*, Alice.' But from experience, Russell knew his wife liked to underline any point she was making with an act.

'Johnny Viagra's got some sweet kissing lips.'

In the Fast lane, here was the breast-stroker, punching through the water with such force she was like an ice-breaker.

Drunk, humiliated, Russell had bum-shuffled to the edge of the bed and swung, catching her just above the knee. He owned it. He'd always owned it. But of course, he also always blamed Eric—if Eric hadn't kissed her, if Eric and Una hadn't been on the trip . . .

The fire burned in a steel box beneath the tub. There was a long narrow gate with a clever latch you used when you needed to feed the flames. Eric stood and the water from his body rained onto the steel, hissing.

'Alice,' he said.

Swaying away in one of the villa's white cloth bathrobes, 'Yes, Eric?' she'd said, mocking his serious voice.

Needing to get to her, he'd sort of fallen out the bath. The Steinlager abandoned. His dick thwacking about on the gravel, the little toe of his right foot stuck, cooking for a moment on the steel box, but all those sensations were forgotten as he reached his arms around her shins, pulled his vibrating self up, and pressed his lips to that bruise.

Like a fish she'd caught—there, wet at her feet. You'd think, with that much desire pumping, his next move would've been obvious. But he couldn't go further. He didn't trust Alice to give herself—just as likely she'd squash him with some humiliation. Plus, Una, his Una, asleep only metres away in the cottage. And then there was the respect he had, even back then, for Russell.

Una dying. Their wedding in Ashburton. Eric Jr's birth. The time the Accord, with him in it, ended up in the harbour. Making that speech in the Octagon to the striking teachers. Eric's big moments. Eric, who was still closer to the bottom of the diving pool than the surface. At the critical moment in his tumble turn his heart had batted itself out of rhythm and instead of kicking towards the surface, his disorientated brain had kicked him down, and so now here he was, flapping about in the depths, watching his life pass.

Ugly husks—people didn't touch the old. Russell saw the kids once or twice a year. A handshake from his sons, a quick hug from his daughter. Alice, if she'd been around, would have made them give him a good squeeze, but if she'd been around it wouldn't have mattered. And these days the grandchildren were too old to go for contact. To them he smelled like dung—to them he was as relevant as a shoe box. Friends? Even the close ones engaged in the same formal way they always had.

One thing you could do was get your hair cut. Russell did it every three weeks. Lying back letting them shampoo and condition, sitting there after in the big chair, with them doing all their lovely scissory fiddle-faddling. But no one at the salon ever gripped him in need, ever held him with love or in sympathy. Never just pressed in to share animal contact. He ate alone, showered alone, woke at night alone, her ice-cold shape beside him.

But here were real people, grabbing a hold. Eric and then the breast-stroker. Her breathing hard, her sort of pressing Eric into Russell and then yelling about an ambulance. 'What were you lot doing? This man's drowning!'

Eric had Russell around the neck. Russell had one arm in Eric's armpit and the other over the lane rope. It was as though Eric was very short and they were dancing. Badly, because their legs were all tangled. Eric's mouth was blue. The breast-stroker was treading water in the middle of the lane, reaching back with her hand as if to make sure they didn't go anywhere.

Now she was using a sarcastic, pretty-please type tone. 'Anyone available to help?'

'Eric?' said Russell. 'Eric?'

Eric's eyes were open. Muscles in his face moved.

Russell could feel the weight of Eric's lower body. It was like holding one of those cause-and-effect steel balls on a string. 'Eric?'

Then there were other bodies in the lane. Other hands around Eric and Russell. 'Grab hold, sir.'

The cleaner was at the side with a pole thing. Russell unravelled from Eric and took hold. The man leaned back against the weight and pulled.

Eric watched one-leg drag Russell to the side of the pool. His feet didn't feel right. He was thirsty. They'd call it a draw.

Acknowledgements

Thank you Fergus Barrowman. Thanks for the clear, kind and personal way you deal with my projects. Both the good and the not so good. Thanks for keeping your publishing house open to the short story form. Thanks to Stephen Stratford for your editing. Thanks to Emma Martin for your close reading and advice. Lawrence Patchett, thanks for all your help with these stories mate. Thanks for the phone calls. Our conversations always inspire me to work harder, to really strain against the task.

Thanks to my friend Fiona Mitford—for your warmth and encouragement. Thanks to my other readers, Claire and Francie and all my 2009 friends.

Thanks to anyone who looked after my kids while I wrote—especially Margaret Dukes and Heather Scott. Two of New Zealand's premier babysitters. Thanks to Dad, Bronwyn, John, Richard and Belinda—fine New Zealanders, great supporters.

To Darryl—thanks for absorbing all my vitriol about Trump and his band of morons.

To my children, this is what Dad does when you are at daycare or with Grandma or out with Mum. When you are older, I hope you'll read it. I hope you'll see the beauty and fun of thought, of words, of stories. I hope you'll look after each other and be loyal, tough, kind and loving. All three of you are magnificent.

Finally, to Elizabeth. Thanks for your counsel, your support, your endless love. Thanks for never suggesting I should find something more useful to do with my time.